"Do You [...] Are Going To Believe We Went From Professional Adversaries To Lovers In A Heartbeat?"

"Lovers, huh? I like the sound of that."

"This isn't a plan." Mariama pulled free, inching her chair back. "It's insanity."

"It's a plan that will work. Everyone will want to hear more about the aloof princess finding romance and playing Good Samaritan at Christmastime."

Her eyes went wide with panic, but she stayed in her seat. She wasn't running. Yet.

Rowan shoved to his feet. "Time for bed."

"Bed?" she squeaked, standing, as well.

He could see in her eyes that she'd envisioned them sharing a bed before this moment. And it gave him a surge of victory.

* * *

Yuletide Baby Surprise
is a Billionaires & Babies novel:

Powerful men...wrapped around
their babies' little fingers

* * *

If you're on Twitter,
tell us what you think of Harlequin Desire!
#harlequindesire

Dear Reader,

I love to write baby stories because, well, I love babies! As a mother of four, I savored each child's precious milestones, moments that flew by in a flurry of years. I've enjoyed drawing on those experiences to create the little ones in my stories.

Writing this book with a baby, however, marked a very special milestone in *my* life. I started this book shortly before the birth of my first grandchild and finished writing *Yuletide Baby Surprise* as we celebrated Christmas with a visit from our granddaughter. Needless to say, it was our best Christmas ever!

May the joy of the season be with each of you as you savor making memories with those dearest to you!

Happy Holidays,

Cathy

Website: catherinemann.com
Facebook: www.facebook.com/CatherineMannAuthor
Twitter: twitter.com/#!/CatherineMann1
Pinterest: pinterest.com/catherinemann/

YULETIDE BABY
SURPRISE

—

CATHERINE MANN

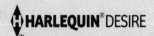

Recycling programs
for this product may
not exist in your area.

ISBN-13: 978-0-373-73270-8

YULETIDE BABY SURPRISE

Copyright © 2013 by Catherine Mann

Printed in U.S.A.

_____

CATHERINE MANN

USA TODAY bestselling author Catherine Mann lives on a sunny Florida beach with her flyboy husband and their four children. With more than forty books in print in over twenty countries, she has also celebrated wins for both a RITA® Award and a Booksellers' Best Award. Catherine enjoys chatting with readers online—thanks to the wonders of the internet, which allows her to network with her laptop by the water! Contact Catherine through her website, www.catherinemann.com, find her on Facebook and Twitter (@CatherineMann1) or reach her by snail mail at P.O. Box 6065, Navarre, FL 32566.

To Savannah

One

Dr. Mariama Mandara had always been the last picked for a team in gym class. With good reason. Athletics? Not her thing. But when it came to spelling bees, debate squads and math competitions, she'd racked up requests by the dozens.

Too bad her academic skills couldn't help her sprint faster down the posh hotel corridor.

More than ever, she needed speed to escape the royal watchers tracking her at the Cape Verde beachside resort off the coast of West Africa, which was like a North Atlantic Hawaii, a horseshoe grouping of ten islands. They were staying on the largest island, Santiago.

No matter where she hid, determined legions were all too eager for a photo with a princess. Why couldn't they accept she was here for a business conference, not socializing?

Panting, Mari braced a hand against the wall as she

stumbled past a potted areca silk palm strung with twinkling Christmas lights. Evading relentless pursuers wasn't as easy as it appeared in the movies, especially if you weren't inclined to blow things up or leap from windows. The nearest stairwell door was blocked by two tourists poring over some sightseeing pamphlet. A cleaning cart blocked another escape route. She could only keep moving forward.

Regaining her balance, she power-walked, since running would draw even more attention or send her tripping over her own feet. Her low-heeled pumps thud-thud-thudded along the plush carpet in time with a poly-rhythmic version of "Hark! The Herald Angels Sing" wafting from the sound system. She just wanted to finish this medical conference and return to her research lab, where she could ride out the holiday madness in peace, crunching data rather than candy canes.

For most people, Christmas meant love, joy and family. But for her, the "season to be jolly" brought epic family battles even twenty years after her parents' divorce. If her mom and dad had lived next door to each other—or even on the same continent—the holidays would not have been so painful. But they'd played trans-continental tug-of-war over their only child for decades. Growing up, she'd spent more time in the Atlanta airport and on planes with her nanny than actually celebrating by a fireside with cocoa. She'd even spent one Christmas in a hotel, her connecting flight canceled for snow.

The occasional cart in the hall now reminded her of that year's room-service Christmas meal. Call her crazy, but once she had gained more control over her world, she preferred a simpler Christmas.

Although simple wasn't always possible for someone

born into royalty. Her mother had crumbled under the pressure of the constant spotlight, divorced her Prince Charming in Western Africa and returned to her Atlanta, Georgia, home. Mari, however, couldn't divorce herself from her heritage.

If only her father and his subjects understood she could best serve their small region through her research at the university lab using her clinical brain, rather than smiling endlessly through the status quo of ribbon-cutting ceremonies. She craved her comfy, shapeless clothes, instead of worrying about keeping herself neat as a pin for photo ops.

Finally, she spotted an unguarded stairwell. Peering inside, she found it empty but for the echo of "Hark! The Herald Angels Sing" segueing into "Away in a Manger." She just needed to make it from the ground level to her fifth-floor room, where she could hole up for the night before facing the rest of the week's symposiums. Exhausted from a fourteen-hour day of presentations about her research on antiviral medications, she was a rumpled mess and just didn't have it in her to smile pretty for the camera or field questions that would be captured on video phone. Especially since anything she said could gain a life of its own on the internet in seconds these days.

She grasped the rail and all but hauled herself up step after step. Urgency pumped her pulse in her ears. Gasping, she paused for a second at the third floor to catch her breath before trudging up the last flights. Shoving through the fifth-floor door, she almost slammed into a mother and teenage daughter leaving their room. The teen did a double take and Mari turned away quickly, adrenaline surging through her exhaustion and powering her down the hall. Except now she was going in the opposite direction, damn it.

Simply strolling back into the hall wasn't an option until she could be sure the path was clear. But she couldn't simply stand here indefinitely, either. If only she had a disguise, something to throw people off the scent. Head tucked down, she searched the hall through her eyelashes, taking in a brass luggage rack and monstrously big pots of African feather grass.

Her gaze landed on the perfect answer—a roomservice cart. Apparently abandoned. She scanned for anyone in a hotel uniform, but saw only the retreating back of a woman walking away quickly, a cell phone pressed to her ear. Mari chewed her lip for half a second then sprinted forward and stopped just short of the cloth-draped trolley.

She peeked under the silver tray. The mouth-watering scent of saffron-braised karoo lamb made her stomach rumble. And the tiramisu particularly tempted her to find the nearest closet and feast after a long day of talking without a break for more than coffee and water. She shook off indulgent thoughts. The sooner she worked her way back to her room, the sooner she could end this crazy day with a hot shower, her own tray of food and a soft bed.

Delivering the room-service cart now offered her best means of disguise. A hotel jacket was even draped over the handle and a slip of paper clearly listed Suite 5A as the recipient.

The sound of the elevator doors opening spurred her into action.

Mari shrugged the voluminous forest-green jacket over her rumpled black suit. A red Father Christmas hat slipped from underneath the hotel uniform. All the better for extra camouflaging. She yanked on the hat over her upswept hair and started pushing the heavily laden cart toward the suite at the end of the hall, just as voices swelled behind her.

"Do you see her?" a female teen asked in Portuguese, her squeaky tones drifting down the corridor. "I thought you said she ran up the stairs to the fifth floor."

"Are you sure it wasn't the fourth?" another high-pitched girl answered.

"I'm certain," a third voice snapped. "Get your phone ready. We can sell these for a fortune."

Not a chance.

Mari shoved the cart. China rattled and the wheels creaked. Damn, this thing was heavier than it looked. She dug her heels in deeper and pushed harder. Step by step, past carved masks and a pottery elephant planter, she walked closer to suite 5A.

The conspiring trio drew closer. "Maybe we can ask that lady with the cart if she's seen her...."

Apprehension lifted the hair on the back of Mari's neck. The photos would be all the more mortifying if they caught her in this disguise. She needed to get inside suite 5A. Now. The numbered brass plaque told her she was at the right place.

Mari jabbed the buzzer, twice, fast.

"Room service," she called, keeping her head low.

Seconds ticked by. The risk of stepping inside and hiding her identity from one person seemed far less daunting than hanging out here with the determined group and heaven only knew who else.

Just when she started to panic that time would run out, the door opened, thank God. She rushed past, her arms straining at the weight of the cart and her nose catching a whiff of manly soap. Her favorite scent—

clean and crisp rather than cloying and obvious. Her feet tangled for a second.

Tripping over her own feet as she shoved the cart was far from dignified. But she'd always been too gangly to be a glamour girl. She was more of a cerebral type, a proud nerd, much to the frustration of her family's press secretary, who expected her to present herself in a more dignified manner.

Still, even in her rush to get inside, curiosity nipped at her. What type of man would choose such a simple smell while staying in such opulence? But she didn't dare risk a peek at him.

She eyed the suite for other occupants, even though the room-service cart only held one meal. One very weighty meal. She shoved the rattling cart past a teak lion. The room appeared empty, the lighting low. Fat leather sofas and a thick wooden table filled the main space. Floor-to-ceiling shutters had been slid aside to reveal the moonlit beach outside a panoramic window. Lights from stars and yachts dotted the horizon. Palms and fruit trees with lanterns illuminated the shore. On a distant islet, a stone church perched on a hill.

She cleared her throat and started toward the table by the window. "I'll set everything up on the table for you."

"Thanks," rumbled a hauntingly familiar voice that froze her in her tracks. "But you can just leave it there by the fireplace."

Her brain needed less than a second to identify those deep bass tones. Ice trickled down her spine as if snow had hit her African Christmas after all.

She didn't have to turn around to confirm that fate was having a big laugh at her expense. She'd run from an irritation straight into a major frustration. Out of all the hotel suites she could have entered, somehow she'd landed in the room of Dr. Rowan Boothe.

Her professional nemesis.

A physician whose inventions she'd all but ridiculed in public.

What the hell was he doing here? She'd reviewed the entire program of speakers and she could have sworn he wasn't listed on the docket until the end of the week.

The door clicked shut behind her. The tread of his footsteps closed in, steady, deliberate, bringing the scent of him drifting her way. She kept her face down, studying his loafers and the well-washed hem of his faded jeans.

She held on to the hope that he wouldn't recognize her. "I'll leave your meal right here then," she said softly. "Have a nice evening."

His tall, solid body blocked her path. God, she was caught between a rock and a hard place. Her eyes skated to his chest.

A very hard, muscle-bound place encased in a white button-down with the sleeves rolled up and the tail untucked. She remembered well every muscular—annoying—inch of him.

She just prayed he wouldn't recognize her from their last encounter five months ago at a conference in London. Already the heat of embarrassment flamed over her.

Even with her face averted, she didn't need to look further to refresh her memory of that too handsome face of his. Weathered by the sun, his Brad Pitt–level good looks only increased. His sandy blond hair would have been too shaggy for any other medical professional to carry off. But somehow he simply appeared too immersed in philanthropic deeds to be bothered with anything as mundane as a trip to the barber.

The world thought he was Dr. Hot Perfection but she simply couldn't condone the way he circumvented rules.

"Ma'am," he said, ducking his head as if to catch her attention, "is there a problem?"

Just keep calm. There was no way for him to identify her from the back. She would rather brave a few pictures in the press than face this man while she wore a flipping Santa Claus hat.

A broad hand slid into view with cash folded over into a tip. "Merry Christmas."

If she didn't take the money, that would appear suspicious. She pinched the edge of the folded bills, doing her best to avoid touching him. She plucked the cash free and made a mental note to donate the tip to charity. "Thank you for your generosity."

"You're very welcome." His smooth bass was too appealing coming from such an obnoxiously perfect man.

Exhaling hard, she angled past him. Almost home free. Her hand closed around the cool brass door handle.

"Dr. Mandara, are you really going so soon?" he asked with unmistakable sarcasm. He'd recognized her. Damn. He was probably smirking, too, the bastard.

He took a step closer, the heat of his breath caressing her cheek. "And here I thought you'd gone to all this trouble to sneak into my room so you could seduce me."

Dr. Rowan Boothe waited for his words to sink in, the possibility of sparring with the sexy princess/research scientist already pumping excitement through his veins. He didn't know what it was about Mariama Mandara that turned him inside out, but he'd given up analyzing the why of it long ago. His attraction to Mari was simply a fact of life now.

Her disdain for him was an equally undeniable fact, and to be honest, it was quite possibly part of her allure.

He grew weary with the whole notion of the world painting him as some kind of saint just because he'd rejected the offer of a lucrative practice in North Carolina and opened a clinic in Africa. These days, he had money to burn after his invention of a computerized medical diagnostics program—a program Mari missed no opportunity to dismiss as faux, shortcut medicine. Funding the clinic hadn't even put a dent in his portfolio so he didn't see it as worthy of hoopla. Real philanthropy involved sacrifice. And he wasn't particularly adept at denying himself things he wanted.

Right now, he wanted Mari.

Although from the look of horror on her face, his half-joking come-on line hadn't struck gold.

She opened and closed her mouth twice, for once at a loss for words. Fine by him. He was cool with just soaking up the sight of her. He leaned back against the wet bar, taking in her long, elegant lines. Others might miss the fine-boned grace beneath the bulky clothes she wore, but he'd studied her often enough to catch the brush of every subtle curve. He could almost feel her, ached to peel her clothes away and taste every inch of her café-au-lait skin.

Some of the heat must have shown on his face because she snapped out of her shock. "You have got to be joking. You can't honestly believe I would ever make a move on you, much less one so incredibly blatant."

Damn, but her indignation was so sexy and yeah, even cute with the incongruity of that Santa hat perched on her head. He couldn't stop himself from grinning.

She stomped her foot. "Don't you dare laugh at me."

He tapped his head lightly. "Nice hat."

Growling, she flung aside the hat and shrugged out of the hotel jacket. "Believe me, if I'd known you were in here, I wouldn't have chosen this room to hide out."

"Hide out?" he said absently, half following her words.

As she pulled her arms free of the jacket to review a rumpled black suit, the tug of her white business shirt against her breasts sent an unwelcome surge of arousal through him. He'd been fighting a damned inconvenient arousal around this woman for more than two years, ever since she'd stepped behind a podium in front of an auditorium full of people and proceeded to shoot holes in his work. She thought his computerized diagnostics tool was too simplistic. She'd accused him of taking the human element out of medicine. His jaw flexed, any urge to smile fading.

If anyone was too impersonal, it was her. And, God, how he ached to rattle her composure, to see her tawny eyes go sleepy with all-consuming passion.

Crap.

He was five seconds away from an obvious erection. He reined himself in and faced the problem at hand— the woman—as a more likely reason for her arrival smoked through his brain. "Is this some sort of professional espionage?"

"What in the hell are you talking about?" She fidgeted with the loose waistband on her tweedy skirt.

Who would have thought tweed would turn him inside out? Yet he found himself fantasizing about pulling those practical clunky shoes off her feet. He would kiss his way up under her skirt, discover the silken inside of her calf...

He cleared his throat and brought his focus up to her heart-shaped face. "Playing dumb does not suit you." He knew full well she had a genius IQ. "But if that's the way you want this to roll, then okay. Were you hoping to obtain insider information on the latest upgrade to my computerized diagnostics tool?"

"Not likely." She smoothed a hand over her swept-back hair. "I never would have pegged you as the conspiracy theorist sort since you're a man of science. Sort of."

He cocked an eyebrow. "So you're not here for information, Mari." If he'd wanted distance he should have called her Dr. Mandara, but too late to go back. "Then why are you sneaking into my suite?"

Sighing, she crossed her arms over her chest. "Fine. I'll tell you, but you have to promise not to laugh."

"Scout's honor." He crossed his heart.

"You were a Boy Scout? Figures."

Before he'd been sent to a military reform school, but he didn't like to talk about those days and the things he'd done. Things he could never atone for even if he opened free clinics on every continent, every year for the rest of his life. But he kept trying, by saving one life at a time, to make up for the past.

"You were going to tell me how you ended up in my suite."

She glanced at the door, then sat gingerly on the arm of the leather sofa. "Royal watchers have been trailing me with their phones to take photos and videos for their five seconds of fame. A group of them followed me out the back exit after my last seminar."

Protective instincts flamed to life inside him. "Doesn't your father provide you with bodyguards?"

"I choose not to use them," she said without explanation, her chin tipping regally in a way that shouted the subject wasn't open for discussion. "My attempt to slip away wasn't going well. The lady pushing this room-service cart was distracted by a phone call. I saw my chance to go incognito and I took it."

The thought of her alone out there had him biting back the urge to chew out someone—namely her father. So what if she rejected guards? Her dad should have insisted.

Mari continued, "I know I should probably just grin for the camera and move on, but the images they capture aren't…professional. I have serious work to do, a reputation to maintain." She tipped her head back, her mouth pursed tight in frustration for a telling moment before she rambled on with a weary shake of her head. "I didn't sign on for this."

Her exhaustion pulled at him, made him want to rest his hands on her drooping shoulders and ease those tense muscles. Except she would likely clobber him with the silver chafing dish on the serving cart. He opted for the surefire way to take her mind off the stress.

Shoving away from the bar, he strode past the cart toward her again. "Poor little rich princess."

Mari's cat eyes narrowed. "You're not very nice."

"You're the only one who seems to think so." He stopped twelve inches shy of touching her.

Slowly, she stood, facing him. "Well, pardon me for not being a member of *your* fan club."

"You genuinely didn't know this was my room?" he asked again, even though he could see the truth in her eyes.

"No. I didn't." She shook her head, the heartbeat throbbing faster in her elegant neck. "The cart only had your room number. Not your name."

"If you'd realized ahead of time that this was my room, my meal—" he scooped up the hotel jacket and Santa hat "—would you have surrendered yourself to the camera-toting brigade out there rather than ask me for help?"

Her lips quivered with the first hint of a smile. "I guess we'll never know the answer to that, will we?" She tugged at the jacket. "Enjoy your supper."

He didn't let go. "There's plenty of food here. You could join me, hide out for a while longer."

"Did you just invite me to dinner?" The light of humor in her eyes animated her face until the air damn near crackled between them. "Or are you secretly trying to poison me?"

She nibbled her bottom lip and he could have sworn she swayed toward him. If he hooked a finger in the vee of her shirt and pulled, she would be in his arms.

Instead, he simply reached out and skimmed back the stray lock of sleek black hair curving just under her chin. "Mari, there are a lot of things I would like to do to you, but I can assure you that poisoning you is nowhere on that list."

Confusion chased across her face, but she wasn't running from the room or laughing. In fact, he could swear he saw reluctant interest. Enough to make him wonder what might happen if…

A whimper snapped him out of his passion fog.

The sound wasn't coming from Mari. She looked over his shoulder and he turned toward the sound. The cry swelled louder, into a full-out wail, swelling from across the room.

From under the room-service cart?

He glanced at Mari. "What the hell?"

She shook her head, her hands up. "Don't look at me."

He charged across the room, sweeping aside the linen cloth covering the service cart to reveal a squalling infant.

Two

The infant's wail echoed in the hotel suite. Shock resounded just as loudly inside of Mari as she stared at the screaming baby in a plastic carrier wedged inside the room-service trolley. No wonder the cart had felt heavier than normal. If only she'd investigated she might have found the baby right away. Her brain had been tapping her with the logic that something was off, and she'd been too caught up in her own selfish fears about a few photos to notice.

To think that poor little one had been under there all this time. So tiny. So defenseless. The child, maybe two or three months old, wore a diaper and a plain white T-shirt, a green blanket tangled around its tiny, kicking feet.

Mari swallowed hard, her brain not making connections as she was too dumbstruck to think. "Oh, my God, is that a baby?"

"It's not a puppy." Rowan washed his hands at the wet-bar sink then knelt beside the lower rack holding the infant seat. He visibly went into doctor mode as he checked the squalling tyke over, sliding his hands under and scooping the child up in his large, confident hands. Chubby little mocha-brown arms and legs flailed before the baby settled against Rowan's chest with a hiccupping sigh.

"What in the world is it doing under there?" She stepped away, clearing a path for him to walk over to the sofa.

"I'm not the one who brought the room service in," he countered offhandedly, sliding a finger into the baby's tiny bow mouth. Checking for a cleft palate perhaps?

"Well, I didn't put the baby there."

A boy or girl? She couldn't tell. The wriggling bundle wore no distinguishing pink or blue. There wasn't even a hair bow in the cap of black curls.

Rowan elbowed aside an animal-print throw pillow and sat on the leather couch, resting the baby on his knees while he continued assessing.

She tucked her hands behind her back. "Is it okay? He or she?"

"Her," he said, closing the cloth diaper. "She's a girl, approximately three months old, but that's just a guess."

"We should call the authorities. What if whoever abandoned her is still in the building?" Unlikely given how long she'd hung out in here flirting with Rowan. "There was a woman walking away from the cart earlier. I assumed she was just taking a cell phone call, but maybe that was the baby's mother?"

"Definitely something to investigate. Hopefully there will be security footage of her. You need to think through what you're going to tell the authorities, review every detail in your mind while it's fresh." He sounded more like a detective than a doctor. "Did you see anyone else around the cart before you took it?"

"Are you blaming this on me?"

"Of course not."

Still, she couldn't help but feel guilty. "What if this is my fault for taking that cart? Maybe the baby wasn't abandoned at all. What if some mother was just trying to bring her child to work? She must be frantic looking for her daughter."

"Or frantic she's going to be in trouble," he replied dryly.

"Or he. The parent could be a father." She reached for the phone on the marble bar. "I really need to ring the front desk now."

"Before you call, could you pass over her seat? It may hold some clues to her family. Or at least some supplies to take care of her while we settle this."

"Sure, hold on."

She eased the battered plastic seat from under the cart, winging a quick prayer of thankfulness that the child hadn't come to some harm out there alone in the hall. The thought that someone would so recklessly care for a precious life made her grind her teeth in frustration. She set the gray carrier beside Rowan on the sofa, the green blanket trailing off the side.

Finally, she could call for help. Without taking her eyes off Rowan and the baby, she dialed the front desk.

The phone rang four times before someone picked up. "Could you hold, please? Thank you," a harried-sounding hotel operator said without giving Mari a chance to shout "No!" The line went straight to Christmas carols, "O Holy Night" lulling in her ear.

Sighing, she sagged a hip against the garland-draped wet bar. "They put me on hold."

Rowan glanced up, his pure blue eyes darkened with an answering frustration. "Whoever decided to schedule a conference at this time of year needs to have his head examined. The hotel was already jam-packed with holiday tourists, now conventioneers, too. Insane."

"For once, you and I agree on something one hundred percent." The music on the phone transitioned to "The Little Drummer Boy" as she watched Rowan cradle the infant in a way that made him even more handsome. Unwilling to get distracted by traveling down that mental path again, she shifted to look out the window at the scenic view. Multicolored lights blinked from the sailboats and ferries.

The Christmas spirit was definitely in full swing on the resort island. Back on the mainland, her father's country included more of a blend of religions than many realized. Christmas wasn't as elaborate as in the States, but still celebrated. Cape Verde had an especially deep-rooted Christmas tradition, having been originally settled by the Portuguese.

Since moving out on her own, she'd been more than happy to downplay the holiday mayhem personally, but she couldn't ignore the importance, the message of hope that should come this time of year. That a parent could abandon a child at the holidays seemed somehow especially tragic.

Her arms suddenly ached to scoop up the baby, but she had no experience and heaven forbid she did something wrong. The little girl was clearly in better hands with Rowan.

He cursed softly and she turned back to face him. He

held the baby in the crook of his arm while he searched the infant seat with the other.

"What?" she asked, covering the phone's mouthpiece. "Is something the matter with the baby?"

"No, something's the matter with the parents. You can stop worrying that some mom or dad brought their baby to work." He held up a slip of paper, baby cradled in the other arm. "I found this note tucked under the liner in the carrier."

He held up a piece of hotel stationary.

Mari rushed to sit beside him on the sofa, phone still in hand. "What does it say?"

"The baby's mother intended for her to be in this cart, in *my* room." He passed the note. "Read this."

Dr. Boothe, you are known for your charity and generosity. Please look over my baby girl, Issa. My husband died in a border battle and I cannot give Issa what she needs. Tell her I love her and will think of her always.

Mari reread the note in disbelief, barely able to process that someone could give away their child so easily, with no guarantees that she would be safe. "Do people dump babies on your doorstep on a regular basis?"

"It's happened a couple of times at my clinic, but never anything remotely like this." He held out the baby toward her. "Take Issa. I have some contacts I can reach out to with extra resources. They can look into this while we're waiting for the damn hotel operator to take you off hold."

Mari stepped back sharply. "I don't have much experience with babies. No experience actually, other than kissing them on the forehead in crowds during photo ops."

"Didn't you ever babysit in high school?" He cradled the infant in one arm while fishing out his cell phone with his other hand. "Or do princesses not babysit?"

"I skipped secondary education and went straight to college." As a result, her social skills sucked as much as her fashion sense, but that had never mattered much. Until now. Mari smoothed a hand down her wrinkled, baggy skirt. "Looks to me like you have Issa and your phone well in hand."

Competently—enticingly so. No wonder he'd been featured in magazines around the globe as one of the world's most eligible bachelors. Intellectually, she'd understood he was an attractive—albeit irritating—man. But until this moment, she hadn't comprehended the full impact of his appeal.

Her body flamed to life, her senses homing in on this moment, on *him*. Rowan. The last man on the planet she should be swept away by or attracted to.

This must be some sort of primal, hormonal thing. Her ticking biological clock was playing tricks on her mind because he held a baby. She could have felt this way about any man.

Right?

God, she hoped so. Because she couldn't wrap her brain around the notion that she could be this drawn to a man so totally wrong for her.

The music ended on the phone a second before the operator returned. "May I help you?"

Heaven yes, she wanted to shout. She needed Issa safe and settled. She also needed to put space between herself and the increasingly intriguing man in front of her.

She couldn't get out of this suite soon enough.

"Yes, you can help. There's been a baby abandoned just outside Suite 5A, the room of Dr. Rowan Boothe."

Rowan didn't foresee a speedy conclusion to the baby mystery. Not tonight, anyway. The kind of person who threw away their child and trusted her to a man based solely on his professional reputation was probably long gone by now.

Walking the floor with the infant, he patted her back for a burp after the bottle she'd downed. Mari was reading a formula can, her forehead furrowed, her shirt half-untucked. Fresh baby supplies had been sent up by the hotel's concierge since Rowan didn't trust anything in the diaper bag.

There were no reports from hotel security or authorities of a missing child that matched this baby's description. So far security hadn't found any helpful footage, just images of a woman's back as she walked away from the cart as Mari stepped up to take it. Mari had called the police next, but they hadn't seemed to be in any hurry since no one's life was in danger and even the fact that a princess was involved didn't have them moving faster. Delays like this only made it more probable the press would grab hold of information about the situation. He needed to keep this under control. His connections could help him with that, but they couldn't fix the entire system here.

Eventually, the police would make their way over with someone from child services. Thoughts of this baby getting lost in an overburdened, underfunded network tore at him. On a realistic level, he understood he couldn't save everyone who crossed his path, but something about this vulnerable child abandoned at Christmas tore at his heart all the more.

Had to be because the kid was a baby, his weak spot.

He shrugged off distracting thoughts of how badly he'd screwed up as a teenager and focused on the present. Issa burped, then cooed. But Rowan wasn't fooled into thinking she was full. As fast as the kid had downed that first small bottle, he suspected she still needed more. "Issa's ready for the extra couple of ounces if you're ready."

Mari shook the measured powder and distilled water together, her pretty face still stressed. "I think I have it right. But maybe you should double-check."

"Seriously, I'm certain you can handle a two-to-one mixture." He grinned at seeing her flustered for the first time ever. Did she have any idea how cute she looked? Not that she would be happy with the "cute" label. "Just think of it as a lab experiment."

She swiped a wrist over the beads of sweat on her forehead, a simple watch sliding down her slim arm. "If I got the proportions wrong—"

"You didn't." He held out a hand for the fresh bottle. "Trust me."

Reluctantly, she passed it over. "She just looks so fragile."

"Actually, she appears healthy, well fed and clean." Her mother may have dumped her off, but someone had taken good care of the baby before that. Was the woman already regretting her decision? God, he hoped so. There were already far too few homes for orphans here. "There are no signs she's been mistreated."

"She seems cuddly," Mari said with a wistful smile.

"Are you sure you wouldn't like to hold her while I make a call?"

She shook her head quickly, tucking a stray strand of hair back into the loose knot at her neck. "Your special contacts?"

He almost smiled at her weak attempt to distract him from passing over the baby. And he definitely wasn't in a position to share much of anything about his unorthodox contacts with her. "It would be easier if I didn't have to juggle the kid and the bottle while I talk."

"Okay, if you're sure I won't break her." She chewed her bottom lip. "But let me sit down first."

Seeing Mari unsure of herself was strange, to say the least. She always commanded the room with her confidence and knowledge, even when he didn't agree with her conclusions. There was something vulnerable, approachable even, about her now.

He set the baby into her arms, catching a whiff of Mari's perfume, something flowery and surprisingly whimsical for such a practical woman. "Just be careful to support her head and hold the bottle up enough that she isn't drinking air."

Mari eyed the bottle skeptically before popping it into Issa's mouth. "Someone really should invent a more precise way to do this. There's too much room for human error."

"But babies like the human touch. Notice how she's pressing her ear against your heart?" Still leaning in, he could see Mari's pulse throbbing in her neck. The steady throb made him burn to kiss her right there, to taste her, inhale her scent. "That heartbeat is a constant in a baby's life in utero. They find comfort in it after birth, as well."

Her deep golden gaze held his and he could swear something, an awareness, flashed in her eyes as they played out this little family tableau.

"Um, Rowan—" her voice came out a hint breathier than normal "—make your call, please."

Yeah, probably a good idea to retreat and regroup while he figured out what to do about the baby—and about having Mari show up unexpectedly in his suite.

He stepped into his bedroom and opened the French door onto the balcony. The night air was that perfect temperature—not too hot or cold. Decembers in Cape Verde usually maxed out at between seventy-five and eighty degrees Fahrenheit. A hint of salt clung to the air and on a normal night he would find sitting out here with a drink the closest thing to a vacation he'd had in... He'd lost count of the years.

But tonight he had other things on his mind.

Fishing out his phone, he leaned on the balcony rail so he could still see Mari through the picture window in the sitting area. His gaze roved over her lithe body, which was almost completely hidden under her ill-fitting suit. At least she wouldn't be able to hear him. His contacts were out of the normal scale and the fewer people who knew about them, the better. Those ties traced back far, all the way to high school.

After he'd derailed his life in a drunk-driving accident as a teen, he'd landed in a military reform school with a bunch of screwups like himself. He'd formed lifetime friendships there with the group that had dubbed themselves the Alpha Brotherhood. Years later after college graduation, they'd all been stunned to learn their headmaster had connections with Interpol. He'd recruited a handful of them as freelance agents. Their troubled pasts—and large bank accounts—gave them a cover story to move freely in powerful and sometimes seedy circles.

Rowan was only tapped for missions maybe once

a year, but it felt damn good to help clean up underworld crime. He saw the fallout too often in the battles between warlords that erupted in regions neighboring his clinic.

The phone stopped ringing and a familiar voice said, "Speak to me, Boothe."

"Colonel, I need your help."

The Colonel laughed softly. "Tell me something new. Which one of your patients is in trouble? Or is it another cause you've taken on? Or—"

"Sir, it's a baby."

The sound of a chair squeaking echoed over the phone lines and Rowan could envision his old headmaster sitting up straighter, his full attention on the moment. "You have a baby?"

"Not *my* baby. *A* baby." He didn't expect to ever have children. His life was too consumed with his work, his mission. It wouldn't be fair to a child to have to compete with third-world problems for his father's attention. Still, Rowan's eyes locked in on Mari holding Issa so fiercely, as if still afraid she might drop her. "Someone abandoned an infant in my suite along with a note asking me to care for her."

"A little girl. I always wanted a little girl." The nostalgia in the Colonel's voice was at odds with the stern exterior he presented to the world. Even his clothes said stark long after he'd stopped wearing a uniform. These days, in his Interpol life, Salvatore wore nothing but gray suits with a red tie. "But back to your problem at hand. What do the authorities say?"

"No one has reported a child missing to the hotel security or to local authorities. Surveillance footage hasn't shown anything, but there are reports of a woman walking away from the cart where the baby was abandoned. The police are dragging their feet on showing up here to investigate further. So I need to get ahead of the curve here."

"In what way?"

"You and I both know the child welfare system here is overburdened to the crumbling point." Rowan found a plan forming in his mind, a crazy plan, but one that felt somehow right. Hell, there wasn't any option that sat completely right with his conscience. "I want to have temporary custody of the child while the authorities look into finding the mother or placing her in a home."

He might not be the best parental candidate for the baby, but he was a helluva lot better than an overflowing orphanage. If he had help…

His gaze zeroed in on the endearing tableau in his hotel sitting room. The plan came into sharper focus as he thought of spending more time with Mari.

Yet as soon as he considered the idea, obstacles piled in his path. How would he sell her on such an unconventional solution? She freaked out over feeding the kid a bottle.

"Excuse me for asking the obvious, Boothe, but how in the hell do you intend to play papa and save the world at the same time?"

"It's only temporary." He definitely couldn't see himself doing the family gig long-term. Even thinking of growing up with his own family sent his stomach roiling. Mari made it clear her work consumed her, as well. So a temporary arrangement could suit them both well. "And I'll have help…from someone."

"Ah, now I understand."

"How do you understand from a continent away?" Rowan hated to think he was that transparent.

"After my wife wised up and left me, when I had our

son for the weekend, I always had trouble matching up outfits for him to wear. So she would send everything paired up for me." He paused, the sound of clinking ice carrying over the phone line.

Where was Salvatore going with this story? Rowan wasn't sure, but he'd learned long ago that the man had more wisdom in one thumb that most people had in their entire brain. God knows, he'd saved and redirected dozens of misfit teenagers at the military high school.

Salvatore continued, "This one time, my son flipped his suitcase and mixed his clothes up. I did the best I could, but apparently, green plaid shorts, an orange striped shirt and cowboy boots don't match."

"You don't say." The image of Salvatore in his uniform or one of those generic suits of his, walking beside a mismatched kid, made Rowan grin. Salvatore didn't offer personal insights often. This was a golden moment and Rowan just let him keep talking.

"Sure, I knew the outfit didn't match, although I didn't know how to fix it. In the end, I learned a valuable lesson. When you're in the grocery store with the kid, that outfit shouts 'single dad' to a bevy of interested women."

"You used your son to pick up women?"

"Not intentionally. But that's what happened. Sounds to me like you may be partaking of the same strategy with this 'someone' who's helping you."

Busted. Although he felt compelled to defend himself. "I would be asking for help with the kid even if Mari wasn't here."

"Mariama Mandara?" Salvatore's stunned voice reverberated. "You have a thing for a local princess?"

Funny how Rowan sometimes forgot about the princess part. He thought of her as a research scientist. A professional colleague—and sometimes adversary. But most of all, he thought of her as a desirable woman, someone he suddenly didn't feel comfortable discussing with Salvatore. "Could we get back on topic here? Can you help me investigate the baby's parents or not?"

"Of course I can handle that." The Colonel's tone returned to all business, story time over.

"Thank you, sir. I can't tell you how much I appreciate this." Regardless of his attraction to Mari, Rowan couldn't lose sight of the fact that a defenseless child's future hung in the balance here.

"Just send me photos, fingerprints, footprints and any other data you've picked up."

"Roger. I know the drill."

"And good luck with the princess," Salvatore said, chuckling softly before he hung up.

Rowan drew in a deep breath of salty sea air before returning to the suite. He hated being confined. He missed his clinic, the wide-open spaces around it and the people he helped in a tangible way rather than by giving speeches.

Except once he returned home in a week to prepare for Christmas, his window of time with Mari would be done. Back to business.

He walked across the balcony and entered the door by the picture window, stepping into the sitting room. Mari didn't look up, her focus totally on the baby.

Seeing Mari in an unguarded moment was rare. The woman kept major walls up, giving off a prickly air. Right now, she sat on the sofa with her arms cradling the baby—even her body seemed to wrap inward protectively around this child. Mari might think she knew nothing about children, but her instincts were good. He'd watched enough new moms in his career to identify the ones who would have trouble versus the ones who sensed the kid's needs.

The tableau had a Madonna-and-child air. Maybe it was just the holidays messing with his head. If he wanted his half-baked plan to work, he needed to keep his head on straight and figure out how to get her on board with helping him.

"How's Issa doing?"

Mari looked up quickly, as if startled. She held up the empty bottle. "All done with her feeding."

"I'm surprised you're still sticking around. Your fans must have given up by now. The coast will be clear back to your room."

Saying that, he realized he should have mentioned those overzealous royal watchers to Salvatore. Perhaps some private security might be in order. There was a time he didn't have the funds for things like that, back in the days when he was buried in the debt of school loans, before he'd gone into partnership with a computer-whiz classmate of his.

"Mari? Are you going back to your room?" he repeated.

"I still feel responsible for her." Mari smoothed a finger along the baby's chubby cheek. "And the police will want to speak to me. If I'm here, it will move things along faster."

"You do realize the odds are low that her parents will be found tonight," he said, laying the groundwork for getting her to stick around.

"Of course, I understand." She thumbed aside a hint of milk in the corner of the infant's mouth. "That doesn't stop me from hoping she'll have good news soon."

"You sure seem like a natural with her. Earlier, you said you never babysat."

She shrugged self-consciously. "I was always busy studying."

"There were no children in your world at all?" He sat beside her, drawing in the scent of her flowery perfume. Curiosity consumed him, a desperate need to know exactly what flower she smelled like, what she preferred.

"My mother and father don't have siblings. I'm the only child of only children."

This was the closest to a real conversation they'd ever exchanged, talk that didn't involve work or bickering. He couldn't make a move on her, not with the baby right here in the room. But he could feel her relaxing around him. He wanted more of that, more of her, this exciting woman who kept him on his toes.

What would she do if he casually stretched his arm along the back of the sofa? Her eyes held his and instead of moving, he stayed stock-still, looking back at her, unwilling to risk breaking the connection—

The phone jangled harshly across the room.

Mari jolted. The baby squawked.

And Rowan smiled. This particular moment to get closer to Mari may have ended. But make no mistake, he wasn't giving up. He finally had a chance to explore the tenacious desire that had been dogging him since he'd first seen her.

Anticipation ramped through him at the thought of persuading her to see this connection through to its natural—and satisfying—conclusion.

Three

Pacing in front of the sitting room window, Mari cradled the baby against her shoulder as Rowan talked with the local police. Sure, the infant had seemed three months old when she'd looked at her, but holding her? Little Issa felt younger, more fragile.

Helpless.

So much about this evening didn't add up. The child had been abandoned yet she seemed well cared for. Beyond her chubby arms and legs, she had neatly trimmed fingernails and toenails. Her clothes were simple, but clean. She smelled freshly bathed. Could she have been kidnapped as revenge on someone? Growing up, Mari had been constantly warned of the dangers of people who would try to hurt her to get back at her father, as well as people would use her to get *close* to her father. Trusting anyone had been all but impossible.

She shook off the paranoid thoughts and focused on

the little life in her arms. Mari stroked the baby's impossibly soft cheeks, tapped the dimple in her chin. Did she look like her mother or father? Was she missed? Round chocolate-brown eyes blinked up at her trustingly.

Her heart squeezed tight in her chest in a totally illogical way. She'd only just met the child, for heaven's sake, and she ached to press a kiss to her forehead.

Mari glanced to the side to see if Rowan had observed her weak moment, but he was in the middle of finishing up his phone conversation with the police.

Did he practice looking so hot? Even in jeans, he owned the room. Her eyes were drawn to the breadth of his shoulders, the flex of muscles in his legs as he shuffled from foot to foot, his loafers expensive but well worn. He exuded power and wealth without waste or conspicuous consumption. How could he be such a good man and so annoying at the same time?

Rowan hung up the phone and turned, catching her studying him. He cocked an eyebrow. She forced herself to stare back innocently, her chin tipping even as her body tingled with awareness.

"What did the police say?" she asked casually, swaying from side to side in a way she'd found the baby liked.

"They're just arriving outside the hotel." He closed the three feet between them. "They're on their way up to take her."

"That's it?" Her arms tightened around Issa. "She'll be gone minutes from now? Did they say where they will be sending her? I have connections of my own. Maybe I can help."

His blue eyes were compassionate, weary. "You and I both already know what will happen to her. She will be sent to a local orphanage while the police use their limited resources to look into her past, along with all the other cases and other abandoned kids they have in their stacks of files to investigate. Tough to hear, I realize. But that's how it is. We do what we can, when we can."

"I understand." That didn't stop the frustration or the need to change things for this innocent child in her arms and all the children living in poverty in her country.

He scooped the baby from her before she could protest. "But that's not how it has to be today. We *can* do something this time."

"What do you mean?" She crossed her empty arms over her chest, hope niggling at her that Rowan had a reasonable solution.

"We only have a few more minutes before they arrive so I need to make this quick." He hefted the baby onto his shoulder and rubbed her back in small, hypnotic circles. "I think we should offer to watch Issa."

Thank heaven he was holding the child because he'd stunned Mari numb. She watched his hand smoothing along the baby's back and tried to gather her thoughts. "Um, what did you say?"

"We're both clearly qualified and capable adults." His voice reverberated in soothing waves. "It would be in the best interest of the child, a great Christmas message of goodwill, for us to keep her."

Keep her?

Mari's legs folded out from under her and she sank to the edge of the leather sofa. She couldn't have heard him right. She'd let her attraction to him distract her. "What did you say?"

He sat beside her, his thigh pressing warm and solid against hers. "We can have temporary custody of her, just for a couple of weeks to give the police a chance to find out if she has biological relatives able to care for her."

"Have you lost your mind?" Or maybe she had lost hers because she was actually tempted by his crazy plan.

"Not that I know of."

She pressed the back of her wrist to her forehead, stunned that he was serious. Concerns cycled through her head about work and the hoopla of a media circus. "This is a big decision for both of us, something that should be thought over carefully."

"In medicine I have to think fast. I don't always have the luxury of a slow and steady scientific exam," he said, with a wry twist to his lips. "Years of going with my gut have honed my instincts, and my instincts say this is the right thing to do."

Her mind settled on his words and while she never would have gotten to that point on her own, the thought of this baby staying with him rather than in some institution was appealing. "So you'll be her temporary guardian?"

"Our case is more powerful if we offer to do this as a partnership. Both of us." His deep bass and logic drew her in. "Think of the positive PR you'll receive. Your father's press corps will be all over this philanthropic act of yours, which should take some pressure off you at the holidays," he offered, so logically she could almost believe him.

"It isn't as simple as that. The press can twist things, rumors will start about both of us." What if they thought it was *her* baby? She squeezed her eyes closed and bolted off the sofa. "I need more time."

The buzzer rang at the door. Her heart went into her throat.

She heard Rowan follow her. Felt the heat of him at her back. Felt the urgency.

"Issa doesn't have time, Mari. You need to decide if you'll do this. Decide to commit now."

She turned sharply to find him standing so close the three of them made a little family circle. "But you could take her on your own—"

"Maybe the authorities would accept that. But maybe not. We should lead with our strongest case. For her." He cradled the baby's head. "We didn't ask for this, but we're here." Fine lines fanned from the corners of his eyes, attesting to years of worry and long hours in the sun. "We may disagree on a lot of things, but we're people who help."

"You're guilt-tripping me," she accused in the small space between them, her words crackling like small snaps of electricity. And the guilt was working. Her concerns about gossip felt absolutely pathetic in light of the plight of this baby.

As much as she gave Rowan hell about his computer inventions, she knew all about his humanitarian work at the charity clinic. He devoted his life to helping others. He had good qualities underneath that arrogant charm.

"Well, people like us who help in high-stakes situations learn to use whatever means are at our disposal." He half smiled, creasing the lines deeper. "Is it working?"

Those lines from worry and work were real. She might disapprove of his methods, but she couldn't question his motivations, his altruistic spirit. Seeing him deftly rock the baby to sleep ended any argument. For this one time at least, she was on his team.

For Issa.

"Open the door and you'll find out."

* * *

Three hours later, Mari watched Rowan close the hotel door after the police. Stacks of paperwork rested on the table, making it official. She and Rowan had temporary custody of the baby while the police investigated further and tried to track down the employee who'd walked away from the cart.

Issa slept in her infant seat, secure for now.

Mari sighed in relief, slumping in exhaustion back onto the sofa. She'd done it. She'd played the princess card and all but demanded the police obey her "request" to care for the baby until Christmas—less than two weeks away—or until more information could be found about Issa's parents. She'd agreed to care for the child with Rowan Boothe, a doctor who'd saved countless young lives. The police had seemed relieved to have the problem resolved so easily. They'd taken photos of the baby and prints. They would look into the matter, but their faces said they didn't hold out much hope of finding answers.

Maybe she should hire a private detective to look deeper than the police. Except it was almost midnight now. Any other plans would have to wait until morning.

Rowan rested a hand on Mari's shoulder. "Would you get my medical bag so I can do a more thorough checkup? It's in the bedroom by my shaving kit. I'd like to listen to her heart."

He squeezed her shoulder once, deliciously so, until her mouth dried right up from that simple touch.

"Medical bag." She shot to her feet. "Right, of course."

She was too tired and too unsettled to fight off the sensual allure of him right now. She stepped into Rowan's bedroom, her eyes drawn to the hints of him everywhere. A suit was draped over the back of a rattan rocker by sliding doors that led out to a balcony. She didn't consider herself a romantic by any stretch but the thought of sitting out there under the stars with someone…

God, what was the matter with her? This man had driven her bat crazy for years. Now she was daydreaming about an under-the-stars make-out session that would lead back into the bedroom. His bedroom.

Her eyes skated to the sprawling four-poster draped with gauzy netting, a dangerous place to look with his provocative glances still steaming up her memories. An e-reader rested on the bedside table, his computer laptop tucked underneath. Her mind filled with images of him sprawled in that massive bed—working, reading—details about a man she'd done her best to avoid. She pulled her eyes away.

The bathroom was only a few feet away. She charged across the plush carpet, pushing the door wide. The scent of him was stronger in here, and she couldn't resist breathing in the soapy aroma clinging to the air— patchouli, perhaps. She swallowed hard as goose bumps of awareness rose on her skin, her senses on overload.

A whimpering baby cry from the main room reminded her of her mission here. She shook off frivolous thoughts and snagged the medical bag from the marble vanity. She wrapped her hands around the well-worn leather with his name on a scratched brass plate. The dichotomy of a man this wealthy carrying such a battered bag added layers to her previously clear-cut image of him.

Clutching the bag to her stomach, she returned to the sitting room. Rowan set aside a bottle and settled the baby girl against his shoulder, his broad palm patting her back.

How exactly were they going to work this baby bargain? She had absolutely no idea.

For the first time in her life, she'd done something completely irrational. The notion that Rowan Boothe had that much power over her behavior rattled her to her toes.

She really was losing it. She needed to finish this day, get some sleep and find some clarity.

From this point forward, she would keep a firmer grip on herself. And that meant no more drooling over the sexy doc, and definitely no more sniffing his tempting aftershave.

Rowan tapped through the images on his laptop, reviewing the file on the baby, including the note he'd scanned in before passing it over to the police. He'd sent a copy of everything to Colonel Salvatore. Even though it was too early to expect results, he still hoped for some news, for the child's sake.

Meanwhile, though, he'd accomplished a freaking miracle in buying himself time with Mari. A week or so at the most, likely more, but possibly less since her staying rested solely on the child. If relatives were found quickly, she'd be headed home. He didn't doubt his decision, even if part of his motivation was selfish. This baby provided the perfect opportunity to spend more time with Mari, to learn more about her and figure out what made her tick. Then, hopefully, she would no longer be a thorn in his side—or a pain in his libido.

He tapped the screen back to the scanned image of the note that had been left with the baby.

Dr. Boothe, you are known for your charity and generosity. Please look over my baby girl, Issa.

My husband died in a border battle and I cannot give Issa what she needs. Tell her I love her and will think of her always.

His ears tuned in to the sound of Mari walking toward him, then the floral scent of her wrapped around him. She stood behind him without speaking and he realized she was reading over his shoulder, taking in the note.

"Loves her?" Mari sighed heavily. "The woman abandoned her to a stranger based on that person's reputation in the press."

"I take it your heart isn't tugged." He closed the laptop and turned to face her.

"My heart is broken for this child—" she waved toward the sleeping infant in the baby seat "—and what's in store for her if we don't find answers, along with a truly loving and responsible family."

"I'm hopeful that my contacts will have some information sooner than the police." A reminder that he needed to make the most of his time with Mari. What if Salvatore called with concrete news tomorrow? He looked over at Mari, imagining being with her, drawing her into his bedroom, so close to where they were now. "Let's talk about how we'll look after the baby here during the conference."

"Now?" She jolted in surprise. "It's past midnight."

"There are things to take care of, like ordering more baby gear, meeting with the hotel's babysitting service." He ticked off each point on his fingers. "Just trying to fill in the details on our plan."

"You actually want to plan?" Her kissable lips twitched with a smile.

"No need to be insulting," he bantered right back, en-

joying the way she never treated him like some freaking
saint just because of where he chose to work. He wasn't
the good guy the press painted him to be just because
he'd reformed. The past didn't simply go away. He still
had debts that could never be made right.

"I'm being careful—finally. Like I should have been
earlier." Mari fidgeted with the hem of her untucked
shirt, weariness straining her face, dark circles under
her eyes. "She's a child. A human being. We can't just
fly by the seat of our pants."

He wanted to haul Mari into his arms and let her
sleep against his chest, tell her she didn't have to be so
serious, she didn't have to take the weight of the world
on her shoulders. She could share the load with him.

Instead, he dragged a chair from the tiny teak table
by the window and gestured for her to sit, to rest. "I'm
not exactly without the means or ability to care for a
child. It's only for a short time until we figure out more
about her past so we don't have to fly by the seat of our
pants." He dragged over a chair for himself as well and
sat across from her.

"How is it so easy for you to disregard the rules?"
She slumped back.

"You're free to go if you wish."

She shook her head. "I brought her in here. She's my
responsibility."

Ah, so she wasn't in a rush to run out the door. "Do
you intend to personally watch over her while details
are sorted out?"

"I can hire someone."

"Ah, that's right. You're a princess with endless resources," he teased, taking her hands in his.

She pulled back. "Are you calling me spoiled?"

He squeezed her fingers, holding on, liking the feel

of her hands in his. "I would never dare insult you, Princess. You should know that well enough from the provocative things I said to you five minutes ago."

"Oh. Okay." She nibbled on her bottom lip, surprise flickering through her eyes.

"First things first." He thumbed the inside of her wrists.

"Your plan?" Her breathing seemed to hitch.

"We pretend to be dating and since we're dating, and we'd be spending this holiday time together anyway, we decided to help with the child. How does that work for a plan?"

"What?" She gasped in surprise. "Do you really think people are going to believe we went from professional adversaries to lovers in a heartbeat?"

He saw her pulse throb faster, ramping up his in response.

"Lovers, huh? I like the sound of that."

"You said—"

"I said dating." He squeezed her hands again. "But I like your plan better."

"This isn't a plan." She pulled free, inching her chair back. "It's insanity."

"A plan that will work. People will believe it. More than that, they will eat it up. Everyone will want to hear more about the aloof princess finding romance and playing Good Samaritan at Christmastime. If they have an actual human interest piece to write about you it will distract them from digging around to create a story."

Her eyes went wide with panic, but she stayed in her seat. She wasn't running. Yet. He'd pushed as far as he could for tonight. Tomorrow would offer up a whole new day for making his case.

He shoved to his feet. "Time for bed."

"Oh, um," she squeaked, standing, as well. "Bed?"

He could see in her eyes that she'd envisioned them sharing a bed before this moment. He didn't doubt for a second what he saw and it gave him a surge of victory. Definitely best to bide his time and wait for a moment when she wasn't skittish. A time when she would be all in, as fully committed as he was to exploring this crazy attraction.

"Yes, Mari, bed. I'll watch the baby tonight and if you're comfortable, we can alternate the night shift."

She blinked in surprise. "Right. The night schedule. Are you sure you can handle a baby at night and still participate in the conference?"

"I'm a doctor. I've pulled far longer shifts with no sleep in the hospital. I'll be fine."

"Of course. Then I'll call the front desk to move me to a larger suite so I'll have enough space for the baby and the daytime sitter."

"No need to do that. This suite is plenty large enough for all of us."

Her jaw dropped. "Excuse me?"

"All of us," he said calmly, holding her with his eyes as fully as he'd held her hand, gauging her every blink. Needing to win her over. "It makes sense if we're going to watch the baby, we should do it together for efficiency. The concierge already sent someone to pack your things."

Her chest rose faster and faster, the gentle curves of her breasts pressing against the wrinkled silk of her blouse. "You've actually made quite a few plans."

"Sometimes flying by the seat of your pants works quite well." Otherwise he never would have had this chance to win her over. "A bellhop will be delivering your luggage shortly along with more baby gear that I ordered."

"Here? The two—three—of us? In one suite?" she asked, although he noticed she didn't say no.

Victory was so close.

"There's plenty of space for the baby. You can have your own room. Unless you want to sleep in mine." He grinned. "You have to know I wouldn't object."

Four

Buttoning up her navy blue power suit the next morning, Mari couldn't believe she'd actually spent the night in Rowan Boothe's hotel suite. Not his room, but a mere wall away. He'd cared for the baby until morning as he'd promised. A good thing, since she needed to learn a lot more before she trusted herself to care for Issa.

She tucked pins into her swept-back hair, but the mirror showed her to be the same slightly rumpled academic she'd always been. While she wasn't a total innocent when it came to men, she wasn't the wild and reckless type who agreed to spend the night in the same suite as a guy she'd never actually dated. She'd expected to toss and turn all night after the confusing turn of events. She couldn't believe she'd agreed.

Yet in spite of all her doubts, she'd slept better than anytime she could remember. Perhaps because the odds of anyone finding her here were next to nil. Her longtime professional feud with him was well-known, and they hadn't yet gone public with this strange idea of joint custody of an abandoned baby. The hotel staff or someone on the police force would likely leak juicy tidbits about the royal family to the press, but it would all be gossip and conjecture until she and Rowan made their official statement verifying the situation.

Soon enough the world would know. Eventually the cameras would start snapping. Her gut clenched at the thought of all those stalkers and the press feeding on the tiniest of details, the least scrap of her life. What if they fed on the innocence of the baby?

Or what if they picked up on the attraction between her and Rowan?

There was still time to back out, write it all off as simple gossip. The urge was strong to put back on that Christmas hat and slip away, to hide in her lab, far, far from the stress of being on show and always falling short. She craved the peace of her laboratory and cubbyhole office, where she truly reigned supreme. Here, in Rowan's suite, she felt so off-kilter, so out of control.

A coo from the other room reminded her she needed to hurry. She stepped away from the mirror and slid her feet into her low, blue pumps. She pulled open her bedroom door, then sagged to rest against the doorjamb. The sight of the little one in a ruffled pink sleeper, resting against Rowan's shoulder, looked like something straight off a greeting card. So perfect.

Except that perfection was an illusion.

Even though Rowan had the baby well in hand, the child was helpless outside their protection. Issa had no one to fight for her, not really, not if Mari and Rowan gave up on her. Even if Mari left and Rowan stayed, he couldn't offer the baby everything Mari could. Her fame—that fame she so resented—could be Issa's salvation.

The baby would get an exposure the police never could have provided. In these days of DNA testing, it wasn't as if fake relatives could step forward to claim a precious infant. So Mari wasn't going anywhere, except to give her presentation at the medical conference, then she'd take the baby for a walk with Rowan.

Looking around the suite strewn with baby paraphernalia, anyone would believe they were truly guardians of the child. Rowan had ordered a veritable nursery set up with top-of-the-line gear. A portable bassinet rested in the corner of the main room, a monitor perched beside it. He'd ordered a swing, a car seat, plus enough clothes, food and diapers for three babies for a month.

He knew what an infant needed, or at least he knew who to call.

Hopefully that call had included a sitter since he was dressed for work as well, in a black Savile Row suit with a Christmas-red tie. God, he was handsome, with his blond hair damp and combed back, his broad hand patting the baby's back. His face wore a perpetual five-o'clock shadow, just enough to be nighttime sexy without sliding over into scruffy.

He filled out the expensive suit with ease. Was there any realm that made this man uncomfortable? He'd taken care of the baby through the night and still looked totally put together.

His eyes searched hers and she shivered, wondering what he saw as he stood there holding Issa so easily. The man was a multitasker. He was also someone with an uncanny knack for getting into a person's mind. He'd found her vulnerable spot in one evening. After all of her tense and bicontinental Christmases, she simply couldn't bear for this child to spend the holidays confused and scared while the system figured out what to do with her—and the other thousands of orphans in their care.

She couldn't replace the child's mother, but she could make sure the child was held, cared for, secure. To do that, she needed to keep her mind off the charismatic man a few feet away.

He looked over at her as if he'd known she was there the whole time. "Good morning. Coffee's ready along with a tray of pastries."

And some sweet, sticky *bouili* dipping sauce.

Her mouth watered for the food almost as much as for the man. She walked to the granite countertop and poured herself a mug of coffee from the silver carafe. She inhaled the rich java fragrance steaming up from the dark roast with hints of fruity overtones. "Did she sleep well?"

"Well enough, just as I would expect from a baby who's experienced so much change," he said, tucking the baby into a swing with expert hands. "The hotel's sending up a sitter for the day. I verified her references and qualifications. They seem solid, so we should be covered through our lecture presentations. Tonight we can take Issa out for dinner and a stroll incognito, kill time while we let the cops finish their initial investigation. If they haven't found out anything by tomorrow, we can go public."

Dinner out? Revealing their plan to the world? Her heart pounded with nerves, but it was too late to go back now. The world would already be buzzing with leaked news. Best to make things official on their own terms.

If Issa's family wasn't found by tomorrow, she would have to call her parents and let them know about her strange partnership with Rowan. First, she had to decide how she wanted to spin it so her parents didn't jump to the wrong conclusions—or try to interfere. This needed to be a good thing for the baby, not just about positive press. She would play it by ear today and call them tonight once she had a firmer idea of what she'd gotten herself into.

Maybe Issa would be back with relatives before supper. A good thing, right?

Rowan started the baby swing in motion. The click-click-click mingled with a low nursery tune.

Mari cleared her throat. "I'll check on Issa during lunch and make sure all's going well with the sitter."

"That's a good idea. Thank you." He cradled a cup in strong hands that could so easily crush the fine china.

She shrugged dismissively. It was no hardship to skip the luncheon. She disliked the idle table chitchat at these sorts of functions anyway. "No big sacrifice. Nobody likes conference lunch food."

Laughing softly, he eyed her over his cup of coffee. "I appreciate your working with me on this."

"You didn't leave me much choice, Dr. Guilt Trip."

His smile creased dimples into his face. "Who'd have thought you'd have a sense of humor?"

"That's not nice." She traced the rim of her cup.

"Neither is saying I coerced you." He tapped the tip of her scrunched nose. "People always have a choice."

Of course he was right. She could always walk, but thinking overlong about her compulsion to stay made her edgy. She sat at the table, the morning sun glistening off the ocean waters outside. "Of course I'm doing this of my own free will, for Issa's sake. It has absolutely nothing to do with you."

"Hello? I thought we weren't going to play games."

She avoided his eyes and sipped her steaming java. "What do you mean, games?"

"Fine. I'll spell it out." He set down his cup on the table and sat beside her, their knees almost touching. "You have made it your life's mission to tear down my research and to keep me at arm's length. Yet you chose to stay here, for the baby, but you and I both know there's more to it than that. There's a chemistry between us, sparks."

"Those sparks—" she proceeded warily "—are just a part of our disagreements."

"Disagreements? You've publically denounced my work. That's a little more than a disagreement."

Of course he wouldn't forget that. "See, sparks. Just like I said."

His eyes narrowed. If only he could understand her point. She only wanted to get past his impulsive, pig-headed mindset and improve his programs.

"Mari, you're damn good at diverting from the topic."

"I'm right on point," she said primly. "This is about our work and you refused to consider that I see things from another angle. You've made it your life's mission to ignore any pertinent input I might have for your technological inventions. I am a scientist."

He scraped a hand over his drying hair. "Then why are you so against my computer program?"

"I thought we were talking about what's best for Issa." She glanced at the baby girl still snoozing in the swing with the lullaby playing.

"Princess, you are making my head spin." He sagged back. "We're here for Issa, but that doesn't mean we can't talk about other things, so quit changing the subject every three seconds. In the interest of getting along better during these next couple of weeks, let's discuss your public disdain for my life's work."

Was he serious? Did he really want to hash that out now? He certainly looked serious, drinking his coffee and downing bites of breakfast. Maybe he was one of those people who wanted to make peace at the holidays in spite of bickering all year round. She knew plenty about that. Which should have taught her well. Problems couldn't be avoided or the resolutions delayed. Best to confront them when given the opening.

"Your program is just too much of a snapshot of a diagnosis, too much of a quick fix. It's like fast-food medicine. It doesn't take into account enough variables." Now she waited for the explosion.

He inhaled a deep breath and tipped back in his chair before answering. "I can see your point. To a degree, I agree. I would welcome the chance to give every patient the hands-on medical treatment of the best clinic in the world. But I'm treating the masses with a skeleton team of medical professionals. That computer program helps us triage in half the time."

"What about people who use your program to cut corners?"

Rowan frowned. "What do you mean?"

"You can't truly believe the world is as altruistic as you? What about the clinics using that program to funnel more patients through just to make more money?"

His chair legs hit the floor, his jaw tightening. "I can't be the conscience for the world," he said in an even tone although a tic had started in the corner of his azure-blue eye. "I can only deal with the problems in front of me. I'm working my tail off to come up with help. Would I prefer more doctors and nurses, PAs and midwives, human hands? Hell, yes. But I make do with what I have and I do what I can so those of us who are here can be as efficient as possible under conditions they didn't come close to teaching us about during my residency."

"So you admit the program isn't optimal?" She couldn't believe he'd admitted to the program's short-comings.

"Really?" He threw up his hands. "That's your take-away from my whole rambling speech? I'm being prac-tical, and you're being idealistic in your ivory tower of research. I'm sorry if that makes you angry to hear."

"I'm not the volatile sort." She pursed her lips tightly to resist the temptation to snap at him for devaluing her work.

Slowly, he grinned, leaning closer. "That's too bad."

"Pardon me?" she asked, not following his logic at all.

"Because when you get all flustered, you're really hot."

Her eyes shot open wide, surprise skittering through her, followed by skepticism. "Does that line really work for you?"

"I've never tried it before." He angled closer until his mouth almost brushed hers. "You'll have to let me know."

Before she could gasp in half a breath of air, he brushed his mouth over hers. Shock quickly turned to something else entirely as delicious tingles shimmered through her. Her body warmed to the feel of him, the newness of his kiss, their first kiss, a moment already burning itself into her memory, searing through her with liquid heat.

Her hand fluttered to his chest, flattening, feeling the steady, strong beat of his heart under her palm matching the thrumming heartbeat in her ears. His kiss was nothing like she would have imagined. She'd expected him to be out of control, wild. Instead, he held her like spun glass. He touched her with deft, sensitive hands, surgeon's hands that knew just the right places to graze, stroke, tease for maximum payoff. Her body thrilled at the caress down her spine that cupped her bottom, bringing her closer.

Already she could feel herself sinking into a spiral of lush sensation. Her limbs went languid with desire. She wanted more of this, more of him, but they were a heartbeat away from tossing away their clothes and inhibitions. Too risky for a multitude of reasons, not the least of which was the possibility of someone discovering them.

Those sorts of exposé photos she absolutely did not want circulating on the internet or anywhere else.

Then, too soon he pulled away. How embarrassing that he was the one to stop since she already knew the kiss had to end. Never had she lost control this quickly.

Cool air and embarrassment washed over her as she sat stunned in her chair. He'd completely knocked the world out from under her with one simple kiss. Had he even been half as affected as she was by the moment? She looked quickly at him, but his back was to her already and she realized he was walking toward the door.

"Rowan?"

He glanced over his shoulder. "The buzzer—" Was that a hint of hoarseness in his voice? "The baby sitter has arrived."

Mari pressed her fingers to her still tingling lips, wondering if a day apart would be enough time to shore up her defenses again before their evening out.

* * *

That evening, Rowan pushed the baby stroller along the marketplace road. Vendors lined the street, and he eyed the place for potential trouble spots. Even with bodyguards trailing them, he kept watch. The baby in the stroller depended on him.

And so did the woman beside him. Mari wore her business suit, without the jacket, just the skirt and blouse, a scarf wrapped over her head and large sunglasses on for disguise, looking like a leggy 1940s movie star.

She strolled beside him, her hand trailing along stalls that overflowed with handwoven cloths and colorful beads. Bins of fresh fruits and vegetables sat out, the scent of roasting turkey and goat carrying on the salty beach breeze. Waves crashed in the distance, adding to the rhythmic percussion of a local band playing Christmas tunes while children danced. Locals and tourists angled past in a crush, multiple languages coming at him in stereo—Cape Verdean Creole, Portuguese, French, English…and heaven knew how many others.

Tonight, he finally had Mari out of the work world and alone with him. Okay, alone with him, a baby, bodyguards and a crush of shoppers.

The last rays of the day bathed Mari in a crimson glow. She hadn't referenced their kiss earlier, so he'd followed her lead on that, counting it a victory that she wasn't running. Clearly, she'd been as turned on as he was. But still, she hadn't run.

With the taste of her etched in his memory, there was not a chance in hell he was going anywhere. More than ever, he was determined to get closer to her, to sample a hell of a lot more than her lips.

But he was smart enough to take his time. This

woman was smart—and skittish. He made his living off reading subtle signs, deciphering puzzles, but this woman? She was the most complex individual he'd ever met.

Could that be a part of her appeal? The mysterious element? The puzzle?

The "why" of it didn't matter so much to him right now. He just wanted to make the most of this evening out and hopefully gain some traction in identifying Issa's family. While they'd gotten a few curious looks from people and a few surreptitiously snapped photos, so far, no one had openly approached them.

He checked left and right again, reconfirming their unobtrusive security detail, ensuring the men were close enough to intervene if needed. Colonel Salvatore had been very accommodating about rounding up the best in the business ASAP, although he still had no answers on the baby's identity. Issa's footprints hadn't come up in any databases, but then the child could have been a home birth, unregistered. Salvatore had insisted he hadn't come close to exhausting all their investigative options yet.

For now, their best lead would come from controlled press exposure, getting the child seen and praying some legit relative stepped up to claim her.

Meanwhile, Rowan finally had his chance to be with Mari, to romance her, and what better place than in this country he loved, with holiday festivities lightening the air. He would have cared for the baby even if Mari had opted out, so he didn't feel guilty about using the child to persuade Mari to stay. He was just surprised she'd agreed so easily.

That gave him pause—and encouragement.

She hesitated at a stall of clay bowls painted with

scenes of everyday life. She trailed her fingers along a piece before moving on to the jewelry, where she stopped for the longest time yet. He'd found her weakness. He wouldn't have pegged her as the type to enjoy those sorts of baubles, but her face lit up as she sifted through beads, necklaces. She seemed to lean more toward practical clothes and loose-fitting suits or dresses. Tonight she wore a long jean jumper and thick leather sandals.

Her hand lingered on the bracelets before she stepped back, the wistfulness disappearing from her golden eyes. "We should find somewhere to eat dinner. The conference food has left me starving for something substantial."

"Point the way. Ladies choice tonight," he said, curious to know what she would choose, what she liked, the way he'd just learned her preferences on the bracelets. Shoppers bustled past, cloth sacks bulging with purchases, everything from souvenirs to groceries.

Instinctively, she moved between the baby stroller and the hurrying masses. "How about we eat at a streetside café while we watch the performances?"

"Sounds good to me." He could keep watch better that way, but then he always kept his guard up. His work with Interpol showed him too well that crime didn't always lurk in the expected places.

He glanced down the street, taking in the carolers playing drums and pipes. Farther down, a group of children acted out the nativity in simple costumes. The sun hadn't gone down yet, so there was less worry about crime.

Rowan pointed to the nearby café with blue tables and fresh fish. "What about there?"

"Perfect, I'll be able to see royal watchers coming."

"Although your fan club seems to have taken a break." He wheeled the stroller toward the restaurant where the waitress instructed them to seat themselves. Issa still slept hard, sucking on a fist and looking too cute for words in a red Christmas sleeper.

Mari laughed, the scarf sliding down off her head, hanging loosely around her neck. "Funny how I couldn't escape photo-happy sorts at the hotel—" she tugged at either end of the silky scarf "—and yet now no one seems to notice me when some notoriety could serve some good."

"Issa's photo has already been released to law enforcement. If nothing comes of it by tomorrow morning, the story will break about our involvement and add an extra push. For now, anyway, the baby and I make good camouflage for you to savor your dinner."

"Mama-flage," she said as he held out her chair for her.

"Nice! I'm enjoying your sense of humor more and more." And he was enjoying a lot more about her as well this evening. He caught the sweet floral scent on her neck as he eased her chair into place.

His mind filled with images of her wearing only perfume and an assortment of the colorful beads from the marketplace. Damn, and now he would be awake all night thinking about the lithe figure she hid under her shapeless suits.

Mari glanced back at him, peering over her sunglasses, her amber eyes reflecting the setting sun. "Is something the matter?"

"Of course not." He took his seat across from her, his foot firmly on the stroller even knowing there were a half-dozen highly trained bodyguards stationed anonymously around them. She might not use them, but he'd made sure to hire a crew for the safety of both Mari and Issa.

The waitress brought glasses and a pitcher of fruit juice—guava and mango—not showing the least sign of recognizing the royal customer she served. This was a good dry run for when they would announce their joint custody publicly.

"What a cute baby," the waitress cooed without even looking at them. "I just love her little red Christmas outfit. She looks like an adorable elf." She toyed with toes in tiny green booties.

"Thank you," Mari said, then mouthed at Rowan, "Mama-flage."

After they'd placed their order for swordfish with *cachupa*—a mixture of corn and beans—Mari leaned back in her chair, appearing far more relaxed than the woman who'd taken refuge in his suite the night before. She eased the sunglasses up to rest on top of her head.

"You look like you've had a couple of servings of grogue." Grogue was a sugar cane liquor drunk with honey that flowed freely here.

"No alcohol for me tonight, thank you." She lifted a hand. "My turn to watch the baby."

"I don't mind taking the night shift if you're not comfortable."

She raised a delicately arched dark eyebrow. "Somewhere in the world, a couple dozen new moms just swooned and they don't know why."

"I'm just trying to be helpful. You have the heavier presentation load."

She stirred sugar into her coffee. "Are you trying to coerce me into kissing you again?"

"As I recall, I kissed you and you didn't object."

She set her spoon down with a decisive clink. "Well, you shouldn't count on doing it again."

"Request duly noted," he replied, not daunted in the least. He saw the speeding of her pulse, the flush of awareness along her dusky skin.

He started to reach for her, just to brush his knuckles along that pulse under the pretense of brushing something aside—except a movement just out of the corner of his eye snagged his attention. Alert, he turned to see an older touristy-looking couple moving toward them.

Mari sat back abruptly, her hand fluttering to her throat. Rowan assessed the pair. Trouble could come in any form, at any age. The bodyguards' attention ramped up as they stalked along the perimeter, closing the circle of protection. Mari reached for her sunglasses. Rowan didn't see any signs of concealed weapons, but he slid his hand inside his jacket, resting his palm on his 9 mm, just in case.

The elderly husband, wearing a camera and a man-purse over his shoulder, stopped beside Mari.

"Excuse us, but would you mind answering a question?" he asked with a thick New Jersey accent.

Was their cover busted? If so, did it really matter that they went public a few hours early? Not for him or the baby, but because he didn't want Mari upset, bolting away from the press, terrified, like the night before.

She tipped her head regally, her shoulders braced as she placed the sunglasses on the table. "Go ahead."

The wife angled in eagerly. "Are the two of you from around here?"

Rowan's mouth twitched. Not busted at all. "Not from the island, ma'am. We both live on the mainland."

"Oh, all right, I see." She furrowed her brow. "Maybe

you can still help me. Where's the Kwanzaa celebration?"

Mari's eyes went wide with surprise, then a hint of humor glinted before her face went politely neutral. "Ma'am, that's an American tradition."

"Oh, I didn't realize." Her forehead furrowed as she adjusted her fanny pack. "I just didn't expect so much Christmas celebration."

Mari glanced at the children finishing up their nativity play and accepting donations for their church. "Africa has a varied cultural and religious heritage. How much of each you find depends on which portion of the continent you're visiting. This area was settled by the Portuguese," she explained patiently, "which accounts for the larger influence of Christian traditions than you might find in other regions."

"Thank you for being so patient in explaining." The wife pulled out a travel guide and passed it to her husband, her eyes staying on Mari. "You look very familiar, dear. Have I seen you somewhere before?"

Pausing for a second, Mari eyed them, then said, "People say I look like the Princess Mariama Mandara. Sometimes I even let folks believe that."

She winked, grinning mischievously.

The older woman laughed. "What a wicked thing to do, young lady. But then I imagine people deserve what they get if they like to sneak photos for the internet."

"Would you like a photo of me with the baby on your phone?" Mari leaned closer to the stroller, sweeping back the cover so baby Issa's face was in clear view. "I'll put on my best princess smile."

"Oh, I wouldn't even know how to work the camera on that new phone our kids gave us for our fiftieth anniversary." She elbowed her husband. "We just use our old Polaroid, isn't that right, Nils?"

"I'm getting it out, Meg, hold on a minute." He fished around inside his man-purse.

Mari extended her arm. "Meg, why don't you get in the photo, too?"

"Oh, yes, thank you. The grandkids will love it." She fluffed her bobbed gray hair with her fingers then leaned in to smile while her husband's old Polaroid spit out picture after picture. "Now you and your husband lean in to pose for one with your daughter."

Daughter? Rowan jolted, the fun of the moment suddenly taking on a different spin. He liked kids and he sure as hell wanted Mari, but the notion of a pretend marriage? That threatened to give him hives. He swallowed down the bite of bile over the family he'd wrecked so many years ago and pretended for the moment life could be normal for him. He kneeled beside Mari and the baby, forcing his face into the requisite smile. He was a good actor.

He'd had lots of practice.

The couple finished their photo shoot, doling out thanks and leaving an extra Polaroid shot behind for them. The image developed in front of him, blurry shapes coming into focus, much like his thoughts, his need to have Mari.

Rowan sank back into his chair as the waitress brought their food. Once she left, he asked Mari, "Why didn't you tell that couple the truth about us, about yourself? It was the perfect opening."

"There were so many people around. If I had, they would have been mobbed out of the photo. When the official story about us fostering the baby hits the news in the morning, they'll realize their photo of a princess is real and they'll have a great story to tell their grandchildren. We still get what we want and they get their cool story."

"That was nice of you to do for them." He draped a napkin over his knee. "I know how much you hate the notoriety of being royalty."

She twisted her napkin between her fingers before dropping it on her lap. "I'm not an awful person."

Had he hurt her feelings? He'd never imagined this boldly confident woman might be insecure. "I never said you were. I think your research is admirable."

"Really? I seem to recall a particular magazine interview where you accused me of trying to sabotage your work. In fact, when I came into your suite with the room-service cart, you accused me of espionage."

"My word choices may have been a bit harsh. The stakes were high." And yeah, he liked seeing her riled up with fire in her eyes. "My work world just doesn't give me the luxury of the time you have in yours."

"I simply prefer life to be on my terms when possible. So much in this world is beyond anyone's control."

Her eyes took on a faraway look that made him burn to reel her back into the moment, to finish the thought out loud so he could keep learning more about what made this woman tick. But she'd already distanced herself from him, deep in thought, looking off down the road at the musicians.

He needed those insights if he expected to get a second kiss—and more from her. But he was beginning to realize that if he wanted more, he was going to have to pony up some confidences of his own. An uncomfortable prospect.

As he looked at Mari swaying absently in time with the music, her lithe body at ease and graceful, he knew having her would be well worth any cost.

Five

Mari soaked in the sound of street music mellowing the warm evening air. The steady beat of the *bougarabou* drum with the players' jangling bracelets enriching the percussion reminded her of childhood days. Back when her parents were still together and she lived in Africa full-time, other than visits to the States to see her maternal grandparents.

Those first seven years of her life had been idyllic—or so she'd thought. She hadn't known anything about the painful undercurrents already rippling through her parents' marriage. She hadn't sensed the tension in their voices over royal pressures and her mother's homesickness.

For a genius, she'd missed all the obvious signs. But then, she'd never had the same skill reading people that she had for reading data. She'd barely registered that her mother was traveling to Atlanta more and more frequently. Her first clue had come near the end when she'd overheard her mom talking about buying a home in the States during their Christmas vacation. They wouldn't be staying with her grandparents any longer during U.S. visits. They would have their own place, not a room with family. Her parents had officially split up and filed for divorce over the holidays.

Christmas music never sounded quite the same to her again, on either continent.

The sway melted away from her shoulders and Mari stilled in her wrought-iron seat. The wind still wound around her as they sat at the patio dining area, but her senses moved on from the music to the air of roasting meat from the kitchen and the sound of laughing children. All of it was almost strong enough to distract her from the weight of Rowan's gaze.

Almost.

She glanced over at him self-consciously. "Why are you staring at me? I must be a mess." She touched her hair, tucking a stray strand back into the twist, then smoothed her rumpled suit shirt and adjusted the silver scarf draped around her neck. "It's been a long day and the breeze is strong tonight."

Since when had she cared about her appearance for more than the sake of photos? She forced her hands back to her lap.

Rowan's tanned face creased with his confident grin. "Your smile is radiant." He waved a broad hand to encompass the festivities playing out around them. "The way you're taking in everything, appreciating the joy of the smallest details, your pleasure in it all is… mesmerizing."

His blue eyes downright twinkled like the stars in the night sky.

Was he flirting with her? She studied him suspiciously. The restaurant window behind him filled with the movement of diners and waiters, the edges blurred by the spray of fake snow. She'd always been entranced by those pretend snowy displays in the middle of a warm island Christmas.

"Joy? It's December, Rowan. The Christmas season of *joy*. Of course I'm happy." She thought fast, desperate to defer conversation about her. Talking about Rowan's past felt a lot more comfortable than worrying about tucking in her shirt, for God's sake. "What kind of traditions did you enjoy with your family growing up?"

He leaned back in his chair, his gaze still homed in solely on Mari in spite of the festivities going on around them. "We did the regular holiday stuff like a tree, carols, lots of food."

"What kind of food?" she asked just as Issa squirmed in the stroller.

He shrugged, adjusting the baby's pacifier until the infant settled back to sleep. "Regular Christmas stuff."

His ease with the baby was admirable—and heart-tugging. "Come on," Mari persisted, "fill in the blanks for me. There are lots of ways to celebrate Christmas and regular food here isn't the same as regular food somewhere else. Besides, I grew up with chefs. Cooking is still a fascinating mystery to me."

He forked up a bite of swordfish. "It's just like following the steps in a chemistry experiment."

"Maybe in theory." She sipped her fruit juice, the blend bursting along her taste buds with a hint of coconut, her senses hyperaware since Rowan kissed her. "Suffice it to say I'm a better scientist than a cook. But back to you. What was your favorite Christmas treat?"

He set his fork aside, his foot gently tapping the

stroller back and forth. "My mom liked to decorate sugar cookies, but my brother, Dylan, and I weren't all that into it. We ate more of the frosting than went on the cookies."

The image wrapped around her like a comfortable blanket. "That sounds perfect. I always wanted a sibling to share moments like that with. Tell me more. Details... Trains or dump trucks? Bikes or ugly sweaters?"

"We didn't have a lot of money, so my folks saved and tucked away gifts all year long. They always seemed a bit embarrassed that they couldn't give us more, but we were happy. And God knows, it's more than most of the kids I work with will ever have."

"You sound like you had a close family. That's a priceless gift."

Something flickered through his eyes that she couldn't quite identify, like gray clouds over a blue sky, but then they cleared so fast she figured she must have been mistaken. She focused on his words, more curious about this man than any she'd ever known.

"At around three-thirty on Christmas morning, Dylan and I would slip out of our bunk beds and sneak downstairs to see what Santa brought." He shared the memory, but the gray had slipped into his tone of voice now, darkening the lightness of his story. "We would play with everything for about an hour, then put it back like we found it, even if the toy was in a box. We would tiptoe back into our room and wait for our parents to wake us up. We always pretended like we were completely surprised by the gifts."

What was she missing here? Setting aside her napkin, she leaned closer. "Sounds like you and your brother share a special bond."

"Shared," he said flatly. "Dylan's dead."

She couldn't hold back the gasp of shock or the empathetic stab of pain for his loss. For an awkward moment, the chorus of "Silver Bells" seemed to blare louder, the happy music at odds with this sudden revelation. "I'm so sorry, Rowan. I didn't know that."

"You had no reason to know. He died in a car accident when he was twenty."

She searched for something appropriate to say. Her lack of social skills had never bothered her before now. "How old were you when he died?"

"Eighteen." He fidgeted with her sunglasses on the table.

"That had to be so horrible for you and for your parents."

"It was," he said simply, still toying with her wide-rimmed shades.

An awkward silence fell, the echoes of Christmas ringing hollow now. She chewed her lip and pulled the first question from her brain that she could scavenge. "Were you still at the military reform school?"

"It was graduation week."

Her heart squeezed tightly at the thought of him losing so much, especially at a time when he should have been celebrating completing his sentence in that school.

Without thinking or hesitating, she pushed aside her sunglasses and covered Rowan's hand. "Rowan, I don't even know what to say."

"There's nothing to say." He flipped his hand, skimming his thumb along the inside of her wrist. "I just wanted you to know I'm trusting you with a part of my past here."

Heat seeped through her veins at each stroke of his thumb across her pulse. "You're telling me about yourself to…?"

His eyes were completely readable now, sensual and steaming over her. "To get closer to you. To let you know that kiss wasn't just an accident. I'm nowhere near the saint the press likes to paint me."

Heat warmed to full-out sparks of electricity arcing along her every nerve ending. She wasn't imagining or exaggerating anything. Rowan Boothe *wanted* her.

And she wanted to sleep with him.

The inescapable truth of that rocked the ground underneath her.

The noise of a backfiring truck snapped Rowan back into the moment. Mari jolted, blinking quickly before making a huge deal out of attacking her plate of swordfish and *cachupa,* gulping coffee between bites.

The sputtering engine still ringing in his ears, Rowan scanned the marketplace, checking the position of their bodyguards. He took in the honeymooners settling in at the next table. The elderly couple that had photographed them earlier was paying their bill. A family of vacationers filled a long stretch of table.

The place was as safe as anywhere out in public.

He knew he couldn't keep Mari and the baby under lock and key. He had the security detail and he hoped Mari would find peace in being out in public with the proper protection. The thought of her being chased down hallways for the rest of her life made him grind his teeth in frustration. She deserved better than to live in the shadows.

He owed little Issa a lot for how she'd brought them together. He was moved by the sensitive side of Mari he'd never known she had, the sweetly awkward humanity beneath the brilliant scientific brain and regal royal heritage.

Leaning toward the stroller, Rowan adjusted the baby's bib, reassured by the steady beat of her little heart. He'd given her a thorough physical and thank God she was healthy, but she was still a helpless, fragile infant. He needed to take care of her future. And he would. He felt confident he could, with the help of Salvatore either finding the baby's family or lining up a solid adoption.

The outcome of his situation with Mari, however, was less certain. There was no mistaking the desire in her golden eyes. Desire mixed with wariness.

A tactical retreat was in order while he waited for the appropriate moment to resume his advances. He hadn't meant to reveal Dylan's death to her, but their talk about the past had lulled him into old memories. He wouldn't let that happen again.

He poured coffee from the earthen pot into his mug and hers. "You must have seen some lavish Christmas celebrations with your father."

Her eyes were shielded, but her hand trembled slightly as she reached for her mug. "My father keeps things fairly scaled back. The country's economy is stabilizing thanks to an increase in cocoa export, but the national treasury isn't flush with cash, by any means. I was brought up to appreciate my responsibilities to my people."

"You don't have a sibling to share the responsibility."

The words fell out of his mouth before he thought them through, probably because of all those memories of his brother knocking around in his gut. All the ways he'd failed to save Dylan's life. If only he'd made different decisions… He forced his attention back into the present, on Mari.

"Both of my parents remarried other people, divorced again, no more kids, though." She spread her hands, sunglasses dangling from her fingers. "So I'm it. The future of my country."

"You don't sound enthusiastic."

"I just think there has to be someone better equipped." She tossed aside the glasses again and picked up her coffee. "What? Why the surprised look? You can't think I'm the best bet for my people. I would rather lock myself in a research lab with the coffeemaker maxed out than deal with the day-to-day events of leading people."

"I think you will succeed at anything life puts in your path." Who had torn down this woman's confidence? If only she saw—believed in—her magnificence. "When you walk in a room, you damn near light up the place. You own the space with your presence, lady."

She blew into her mug of coffee, eyeing him. "Thanks for the vote of confidence. But people and all their intangibles like 'magnificence' are beyond me. I like concrete facts."

"I would say some people would appreciate logic in a leader."

She looked away quickly, busying herself with adjusting the netting around the baby's stroller. "I wasn't always this way."

"What do you mean?"

"So precise." She darted a quick glance at him out of the corner of her eye. "I was actually a very scatter-brained child. I lost my hair ribbons in hotels, left my doll or book on the airplane. I was always oversleeping or sluggish in the morning, running late for important events. The staff was given instructions to wake me up a half hour ahead of time."

His mom had woken him and Dylan up through elementary school, then bought them an alarm clock—a really obnoxious clock that clanged like a cowbell. No one overslept. "Did this happen in your mother's or your father's home?"

"Both places. My internal clock just wasn't impressed by alarms or schedules."

She was a kid juggling a bicontinental lifestyle, the pressures of royal scrutiny along with the social awkwardness of being at least five grades ahead of her peers.

When did she ever get to relax? "Sounds to me like you traveled quite a bit in your life. I'm sure you know that losing things during travel is as common as jet lag, even for adults."

"You're kind to make excuses." She brushed aside his explanation. "I just learned to make lists and structure my world more carefully."

"Such as?" he asked, suddenly finding the need to learn more about what shaped her life every bit as important as tasting her lips again.

"Always sitting in the same seat on an airplane. Creating a routine for the transatlantic trips, traveling at the same time." She shrugged her elegant shoulders. "The world seemed less confusing that way."

"Confusing?" he repeated.

She chewed her bottom lip, which was still glistening from a sip of coffee. "Forget I said anything."

"Too late. I remember everything you say." And what a time to realize how true that was.

"Ah, you're one of those photographic-memory sorts. I imagine that helps with your work."

"Hmm…" Not a photographic memory, except when it came to her. But she didn't need to know that.

"I'm sure my routines sound a bit overboard to you. But my life feels crazy most of the time. I'm a princess.

There's no escaping that fact." She set her mug down carefully. "I have to accept that no matter how many lists I make, my world will never be predictable."

"Sometimes unpredictable has its advantages, as well." He ached to trace the lines of her heart-shaped face and finish with a tap to her chin.

Her throat moved in a long swallow. "Is this where you surprise me with another kiss?"

He leaned in, a breath away, and said, "I was thinking this time you could surprise me."

She stared back at him so long he was sure she would laugh at him for suggesting such a thing, especially out in public. Not that the public problem bothered the honeymooners at the next table. Just when Rowan was certain she would tell him to go to hell—

Mari kissed him. She closed those last two inches between them and pressed her lips to his. Closemouthed but steady. He felt drunk even though he hadn't had anything but coffee and fruit juice all evening. The same drinks he tasted on Mari's lips. Her hands, soft and smooth, covered his on the table. Need, hard and insistent, coursed through his body over an essentially simple kiss with a table between them.

And just that fast, she let go, pushing on his chest and dropping back into her chair.

A flush spread from her face down the vee of her blouse. "That was not… I didn't mean…"

"Shhh." He pressed a finger to her lips, confidence singing through him along with the hammering pulse of desire. "Some things don't need to be analyzed. Some things simply are. Let's finish supper so we can turn in early."

"Are you propositioning me?" Her lips moved under his finger.

Deliberately seductive? Either way, an extra jolt of want shot through him, a want he saw echoed in her eyes.

He spread his arms wide. "Why would you think that?" he asked with a hint of the devil in his voice. "I want to turn in early. It's your night with the baby."

The tension eased from her shoulders and she smiled back, an ease settling between them as they bantered. God, she was incredible, smart and lithe, earnest and exotic all at once. He covered her hand with his—

A squeal from the next table split the air. "Oh, my God, it's her." The honeymooner at the next table tapped her husband's arm insistently. "That princess… Mariama! I want a picture with her. Get me a photo, pretty please, pookie."

Apparently the mama-flage had stopped working. They didn't have until the morning for Mari to become comfortable with the renewed public attention. The story about them taking care of a baby—*together*—was about to leak.

Big-time.

Two hours later, Mari patted Issa's back in the bassinet to be sure she was deeply asleep then flopped onto the bed in the hotel suite she shared with Rowan.

Alone in her bedroom.

Once that woman shouted to the whole restaurant that a princess sat at the next table, the camera phones started snapping before her head could stop reeling from that impulsive kiss. A kiss that still tingled all the way to the roots of her hair.

Rowan had handled the curious masses with a simple explanation that they were watching a baby in foster care. More information would be forthcoming at a morning press conference. Easy as pie.

Although she was still curious as to where all the bodyguards had come from. She intended to confront her father about that later and find out why he'd decided to disregard her wishes now of all times.

Granted, she could see the wisdom in a bit more protection for Issa's sake and she liked to think she would have arranged for something tomorrow...on a smaller scale. The guards had discreetly escorted her from the restaurant, along with Rowan and the baby, and all the way back to the hotel. No ducking into bathrooms or racing down hallways. Just a wall of protection around her as Rowan continued to repeat with a smile and a firm tone, "No further comment tonight."

Without question, the papers would be buzzing by morning. That press conference would be packed. Her father's promo guru couldn't have planned it better.... Had Rowan known that when they kissed? Did he have an agenda? She couldn't help but wonder since most people in her life had their own agendas—with extras to spare.

This was not the first time the thought had come to her. By the time she'd exited the elevator, she was already second-guessing the kiss, the flirting, the whole crazy plan. She knew that Rowan wanted her. She just couldn't figure out why.

Until she had more answers, she couldn't even consider taking things further.

She sat up again, swinging her legs off the side of the bed. Besides, she had a baby to take care of and a phone call to make. Since Issa still slept blissfully in the lacy bassinet after her bottle, Mari could get to that other pressing concern.

Her father.

She swiped her cell phone off the teak end table and thumbed auto-dial…two rings later, a familiar voice answered and Mari blurted out, "Papa, we need to talk…."

Her father's booming laugh filled the earpiece. "About the boyfriend and the baby you've been hiding from me?"

Mari squeezed her eyes shut, envisioning her lanky father sprawled in his favorite leather chair on the lanai, where he preferred to work. He vowed he felt closer to nature out there, closer to his country, even though three barriers of walls and guards protected him.

Sighing, she pressed two fingers to her head and massaged her temples. "How did you hear about Rowan and Issa? Have you had spies watching me? And why did you assign bodyguards without consulting me?"

"One question at a time, daughter dear. First, I heard about your affiliation with Dr. Boothe and the baby on the internet. Second, I do not spy on my family—not often, anyway. And third, whatever bodyguards you're referring to, they're not mine. I assume they're on your boyfriend's payroll."

Her head throbbed over Rowan hiring bodyguards without consulting her. Her life was snowballing out of control.

"He's not my boyfriend—" even though they'd kissed and she'd enjoyed the hell out of it "—and Issa is not our baby. She's a foster child, just like Rowan said at the restaurant."

Even though her heart was already moved beyond measure by the chubby bundle sleeping in the frilly bassinet next to her bed.

"I know the baby's not yours, Mariama."

"The internet strikes again?" She flopped back, rolling to her side and holding a pillow to her stomach as she monitored the steady rise and fall of Issa's chest as she slept.

"I keep tabs on you, daughter dear. You haven't been pregnant and you've never been a fan of Rowan Boothe."

An image flashed in her mind of Rowan pacing the sitting room with Issa in his arms. "The baby was abandoned in Dr. Boothe's hotel room and we are both watching over her while the authorities try to find her relatives. You know how overburdened Africa is with orphans. We just couldn't let her go into the system when we had the power to help her."

"Hmm…" The sound of him clicking computer keys filtered through the phone line—her father never rested, always worked. He took his position as leader seriously, no puppet leadership role for him. "And why are you working with a man you can't stand to help a child you've never met? He could have taken care of this on his own."

"I'm a philanthropist?"

"True," her dad conceded. "But you're also a poor liar. How did the child become your responsibility?"

She'd never been able to get anything past her wily father. "I was trying to get away from a group of tourists trying to steal a photo of me at the end of a very long day. I grabbed a room-service tray and delivered it." The whole crazy night rolled through her mind again and she wondered what had possessed her to act so rashly. Never, though, could she have foreseen how it would end. "Turns out it was for Rowan Boothe and there was an abandoned baby inside. There's nothing going on between us."

A squawk from Issa sent her jolting upright again to

pat the baby's back. An instant later, a tap sounded on the door from the suite beyond. She covered the mouthpiece on the phone. "We're okay."

Still, the bedroom door opened, a quizzical look on Rowan's face. "Everything all right?"

"I've got it." She uncovered the phone. "Dad, I need to go."

Rowan lounged against the doorjamb, his eyes questioning. Pressing the phone against her shoulder to hold it to her ear, she tugged her skirt over her knees, curling her bare toes.

"Mari, dear," her father said, "I do believe you have gotten better at lying after all. Seems like there's a lot going on in your life I don't know about."

Her pulse sped up, affirming her father was indeed right. This wasn't just about Issa. She was lying to herself in thinking there was nothing more going on with Rowan. His eyes enticed her from across the room, like a blue-hot flame drawing a moth.

But her father waited on the other end of the line. Best to deflect the conversation, especially while the object of her current hormonal turmoil stood a few feet away. "You should be thrilled about this whole setup. It will make for great publicity, a wonderful story for your press people to spin over the holidays. Papa, for once I'm not a disappointment."

Rowan scowled and Mari wished she could call back the words that had somehow slipped free. But she felt the weight of the knowledge all the same. The frustration of never measuring up to her parents' expectations.

"Mari, dear," her father said, his voice hoarse, "you have never been a disappointment."

A bittersweet smile welled from the inside out.

"You're worse at lying than I am. But I love you anyway. Good night, Papa."

She thumped the off button and swung her bare feet to the floor. Her nerves were a jangled mess from the emotions stirred up by talking to her dad…not to mention the smoldering embers from kissing Rowan. The stroke of his eyes over her told her they were a simple step, a simple word away from far more than a kiss.

But those tangled nerves and mixed-up feelings also told her this was not the time to make such a momentous decision. Too much was at stake, the well-being of the infant in their care…

And Mari's peace of mind. Because it would be far too easy to lose complete control when it came to this man.

Six

Refusing to back down from Rowan's heated gaze, Mari stiffened her spine and her resolve, closing the last three feet between them. "Why did you order body-guards without consulting me?"

He frowned. "Where did you think they'd come from?"

"My father."

"I just did what he should have. I made sure to look after your safety," he said smoothly, arrogantly.

Her chin tipped defiantly. He might have been right about them needing bodyguards—for Issa's sake—but she wasn't backing down on everything. "Just because I kissed you at the restaurant does *not* mean I intend to invite you into my bed."

Grinning wickedly, he clamped a hand over his heart. "Damn. My spirit is crushed."

"You're joking, of course." She stopped just shy of

touching him, the banter sparkling through her like champagne bubbles.

"Possibly. But make no mistake, I do want to sleep with you and every day I wait is…torture." The barely restrained passion in his voice sent those intoxicating bubbles straight to her head. "I'm just reasonable enough to accept it isn't going to happen tonight."

"And if it never happens?" she asked, unwilling to let him know how deeply he affected her.

"Ah, you said 'if.'" He flicked a loose strand of hair over her shoulder, just barely skimming his knuckles across her skin. "Princess, that means we're already halfway to naked."

Before she could find air to breathe, he backed away, slowly, deliberately closing the door after him.

And she'd thought her nerves were a tangled, jangled mess before. Her legs folded under her as she dropped to sit on the edge of the bed.

A suddenly very cold and empty bed.

Rowan walked through the hotel sliding doors that led out to the sprawling shoreline. The cool night breeze did little to ease the heat pumping through his body. Leaving Mari alone in her hotel room had been one of the toughest things he'd ever done, but he'd had no choice for two reasons.

First, it was too soon to make his move. He didn't want to risk Mari changing her mind about staying with him. She had to be sure—very sure—when they made love.

Second reason he'd needed to put some distance between himself and her right now? He had an important meeting scheduled with an Interpol contact outside the hotel. An old school friend of his and the person responsible for their security detail tonight.

Rowan jogged down the long steps from the pool area to the beach. Late-night vacationers splashed under the fake waterfall, others floated, some sprawled in deck loungers with drinks, the party running deep into the night.

His appointment would take place in cabana number two, away from prying eyes and with the sound of the roaring surf to cover conversation. His loafers sank into the gritty sand, the teak shelter a dozen yards away, with a grassy roof and canvas walls flapping lightly in the wind. Ships bobbed on the horizon, lights echoing the stars overhead.

Rowan swept aside the fabric and stepped inside. "Sorry I'm late, my friend."

His old school pal Elliot Starc lounged in a recliner under the cabana in their designated meeting spot as planned, both loungers overlooking the endless stretch of ocean. "Nothing better to do."

Strictly speaking that couldn't be true. The freelance Interpol agent used his job as a world-renowned Formula One race-car driver to slip in and out of countries without question. He ran in high-powered circles. But then that very lifestyle was the sort their handler, Colonel Salvatore, capitalized on—using the tarnished reputations of his old students to gain access to underworld types.

Of course, Salvatore gave Rowan hell periodically for being a do-gooder. Rowan winced. The label pinched, a poor fit at best. "Well, thanks all the same for dropping everything to come to Cape Verde."

Elliot scratched his hand over his buzzed short hair. "I'm made of time since my fiancée dumped me."

"Sorry about that." Talk about headline news. Elliot's past—his vast past—with women, filled headlines across multiple continents. The world thought that's what had broken up the engagement, but Rowan suspected the truth. Elliot's fiancée had been freaked out by the Interpol work. The job had risked more than one relationship for the Brotherhood.

What would Mari think if she knew?

"Crap happens." Elliot tipped back a drink, draining half of the amber liquid before setting the cut crystal glass on the table between them. "I'd cleared my schedule for the honeymoon. When we split I gave her the tickets since the whole thing was my fault anyway. She and her 'BFF' are skiing in the Alps as we speak. I might as well be doing something productive with my time off."

Clearly, Elliot wouldn't want sympathy. Another drink maybe. He looked like hell, dark circles under his eyes. From lack of sleep most likely. But that didn't explain the nearly shaved head.

"Dude, what happened to you?" Rowan asked, pointing to the short cut.

Elliot's curly mop had become a signature with his fans who collected magazine covers. There were even billboards and posters.... All their pals from the military academy—the ones who'd dubbed themselves the Alpha Brotherhood—never passed up an opportunity to rib Elliot about the underwear ad.

Elliot scratched a hand over his shorn hair. "I had a wreck during a training run. Bit of a fire involved. Singed my hair."

Holy hell. "You caught on fire?"

Elliot grinned. "Just my hair."

"How did I miss hearing about that?"

"No need. It's not a big deal."

Rowan shook his head. "You are one seriously messed-up dude."

But then all his former classmates were messed up in some form. Came with the territory. The things that had landed them in that reform school left them with baggage long after graduation.

"You're the one who hangs out in war-torn villages passing out vaccinations and blankets for fun."

"I'm not trailed by groupies." He shuddered.

"They're harmless most of the time."

Except when they weren't. The very reason he'd consulted with Elliot about the best way to protect Mari and Issa. "I can't thank you enough, brother, for overseeing the security detail. They earned their pay tonight."

"Child's play. So to speak." Elliot lifted his glass again, draining the rest with a wince. "What's up with your papa-and-the-princess deal?"

"The kid needed my help. So I helped."

"You've always been the saint. But that doesn't explain the princess."

Rowan ignored the last part of Elliot's question. "What's so saintly about helping out a kid when I have unlimited funds and Interpol agents at my disposal? Saintly is when something's difficult to do."

"And the woman—the princess?" his half-drunk buddy persisted. "She had a reputation for being very difficult on the subject of Dr. Rowan Boothe."

Like the time she'd written an entire journal piece pointing out potential flaws in his diagnostics program. Sure, he'd made adjustments after reading the piece, but holy hell, it would have been nice—and more expedient—if she'd come to him first. "Mari needs my help, too. That's all it is."

Elliot laughed. "You are so damn delusional."

A truth. And an uncomfortable one.

Beyond their cabana tent, a couple strolled arm-in-arm along the shoreline, sidestepping as a jogger sprinted past with a loping dog.

"If you were a good friend you would let me continue with my denial."

"Maybe I'm wrong." Elliot lifted the decanter and refilled his glass. "It's not denial if you acknowledge said problem."

"I am aware of that fact." His unrelenting desire for Mari was a longtime, ongoing issue he was doing his damnedest to address.

"What do you intend to do about your crush on the princess?"

"Crush? Good God, man. I'm not in junior high."

"Glad you know that. What's your plan?"

"I'm figuring that out as I go." And even if he had one, he wasn't comfortable discussing details of his—feelings?—his attraction.

"What happens if this relationship goes south? Her father has a lot of influence. Even though you're not in his country, his region still neighbors your backyard. That could be...uncomfortable."

Rowan hadn't considered that angle and he should have. Which said a lot for how much Mari messed with his mind. "Let me get this straight, Starc. *You* are doling out relationship advice?"

"I'm a top-notch source when it comes to all the wrong things to do in a long-term relationship." He lifted his glass in toast. "Here's to three broken engagements and counting."

"Who said I'm looking for long-term?"

Elliot leveled an entirely sober stare his way, holding for three crashes of the waves before he said, "You truly are delusional, dude."

"That's not advice."

"It is if you really think about it."

He'd had enough of this discussion about Mari and the possibility of a train wreck of epic proportions. Rowan shoved off the lounger, his shoes sinking in the sand. "Good night."

"Hit a sore spot, did I?" Still, Starc pushed.

"I appreciate your…concern. And your help." He clapped Elliot on the shoulder before sweeping aside the canvas curtain. "I need to return to the hotel."

He'd been gone long enough. As much as he trusted Elliot's choice of guards, he still preferred to keep close.

Wind rolled in off the water, tearing at his open shirt collar as he made his way back up the beach toward the resort. Lights winked from trees. Fake snow speckled windows. Less than two weeks left until Christmas. He would spend the day at his house by the clinic, working any emergency-room walk-ins as he did every year. What plans did Mari have? Would she go to her family?

His parents holed up on Christmas, and frankly, he preferred it that way. Too many painful memories for all of them.

He shut off those thoughts as he entered the resort again. Better to focus on the present. One day at a time. That's the way he'd learned to deal with the crap that had gone down. And right now, his present was filled with Mari and Issa.

Potted palms, carved masks and mounted animal heads passed in a blur as he made his way back to his suite. He nodded to the pair of guards outside the door before stepping inside.

Dimmed lights from the wet bar bathed the sitting

area in an amber glow. Silence echoed as he padded his
way to Mari's room. No sounds came from her room
this time, no conversation with her royal dad.

The door to Mari's room was ajar and he nudged it
open slowly, pushing back thoughts of invading her privacy. This was about safety and checking on the baby.

Not an insane desire to see what Mari looked like
sleeping.

To appease his conscience, he checked the baby first
and found the chubby infant sleeping, sucking on her
tiny fist as she dreamed. Whatever came of his situation with Mari, they'd done right by this baby. They'd
kept at least one child safe.

One day at a time. One life saved at a time. It's how
he lived. How he atoned for the unforgivable in his past.

Did Issa's mother regret abandoning her child? The
note said she wanted her baby in the care of someone
like him. But there was no way she could have known
the full extent of the resources he had at his disposal
with Interpol. If so, she wouldn't have been as quick to
abandon her child to him because he could and would
find the mother. It wasn't a matter of if. Only a matter of when.

He wouldn't give up. This child's future depended
on finding answers.

All the more reason to tread carefully with Mari. He
knew what he wanted, but he'd failed to take into con-
sideration how much of a help she would be. How much
it would touch his soul seeing her care for the baby.
From her initial reaction to the baby, he'd expected her
to be awkward with the child, all technical and analytical. But she had an instinct for children, a tenderness in
her heart that overcame any awkwardness. A softness
that crept over her features.

Watching her sleep now, he could almost forget the way Mari had cut him down to size on more than one occasion in the past. Her hair was down and loose on her pillow, black satin against the white Egyptian cotton pillowcase. Moonlight kissed the curve of her neck, her chest rising and falling slowly.

He could see a strap of creamy satin along her shoulder. Her nightgown? His body tightened and he considered scooping her up and carrying her to his room. To hell with waiting. He could persuade her.

But just as he started to reach for her, his mind snagged on the memory of her talking about how she felt like she'd been a disappointment to her family. The notion that anyone would think this woman less than amazing floored him. He might not agree with her on everything, but he sure as hell saw her value.

Her brilliance of mind and spirit.

He definitely needed to stick to his original plan. He would wait. He couldn't stop thinking about that snippet of her phone conversation with her father. He understood that feeling of inadequacy all too well. She deserved better.

Rather than some half-assed seduction, he needed a plan. A magnificent plan to romance a magnificent woman. The work would be well worth the payoff for both of them.

He backed away from her bed and reached for his cell phone to check in with Salvatore. Pausing at the door, he took in the sight of her, imprinting on his brain the image of Mari sleeping even though that vision ensured *he* wouldn't be sleeping tonight.

Mari's dreams filled with Rowan, filled with his blue eyes stroking her. With his hands caressing her as they floated together in the surf, away from work and responsibilities. She'd never felt so free, so languid, his kisses and touches melting her bones. Her mind filled with his husky whispers of how much he wanted her. Even the sound of his voice stoked her passion higher, hotter, until she ached to wrap her legs around his waist and be filled with his strength.

She couldn't get enough of him. Years of sparring over their work, and even the weather if the subject came up… Now all those frustrating encounters exploded into a deep need, an explosive passion for a man she could have vowed she didn't even like.

Although like had nothing to do with this raw arousal—she felt a need that left her hot and moist between the legs until she squirmed in her bed.

Her bed.

Slowly, her dream world faded as reality interjected itself with tiny details, like the slither of sheets against her skin. The give of the pillow as her head thrashed back and forth. The sound of the ocean outside the window—and the faint rumble of Rowan's voice beyond her door.

She sat upright quickly.

Rowan.

No wonder she'd been dreaming of him. His voice had been filtering into her dream until he took it over. She clutched the puffy comforter to her chest and listened, although the words were indistinguishable. From the periodic silences, he must be talking to someone on the phone.

Mari eased from the bed, careful not to wake the baby. She pulled her robe from over a cane rocking chair and slipped her arms into the cool satin. Her one decadent pleasure—sexy peignoir sets. They made her feel like a silver-screen star from the forties, complete with furry kitten-heel slippers, not so high as to trip her up, but still ultrafeminine.

Would Rowan think them sexy or silly if he noticed them? God, he was filling up her mind and making her care about things—superficial things—that shouldn't matter. Even more distressing, he made her want to climb back into that dream world and forget about everything else.

Her entire focus should be on securing Issa's future. Mari leaned over the lace bassinet to check the infant's breathing. She pressed a kiss to two fingers and skimmed them over Issa's brow, affection clutching her heart. How could one little scrap of humanity become so precious so fast?

Rowan's voice filtered through the door again and piqued her curiosity. Who could he be talking with so late at night? Common sense said it had to be important, maybe even about the baby.

Her throat tightened at the thought of news about Issa's family, and she wasn't sure if the prospect made her happy or sad. She grasped the baby monitor receiver in her hand.

Quietly, she opened the door, careful not to disturb his phone conversation. And yes, she welcomed the opportunity to look at Rowan for a moment, a double-edged pleasure with the heat of her dream still so fresh in her mind. He stood with his back to her, phone pressed to his ear as he faced the picture window, shutters open to reveal the moonlit shoreline.

She couldn't have stopped herself if she tried. And she didn't try. Her gaze skated straight down to his butt. A fine butt, the kind that filled out jeans just right and begged a woman to tuck her hand into his back pocket.

Why hadn't she noticed that about him before? Perhaps because he usually wore his doctor's coat or a suit.

The rest of him, though, was wonderfully familiar. What a time to realize she'd stored so much more about him in her memory than just the sexy glide of his blond hair swept back from his face, his piercing blue eyes, his strong body.

Her fingers itched to scale the expanse of his chest, hard muscled in a way that spoke of real work more than gym time with a personal trainer. Her body responded with a will of its own, her breasts beading in response to just the sight of him, the promise of pleasure in that strong, big body of his.

Were the calluses on his hand imagined in her dream or real? Right now it seemed the most important thing in the world to know, to find out from the ultimate test— his hands on her bare flesh.

His back still to her, he nodded and hmmed at something in the conversation, the broad column of his neck exposed, then he disconnected his call.

Anticipation coursed through her, but she schooled her face to show nothing as he turned.

He showed no surprise at seeing her, his moves smooth and confident. He placed his phone on the wet bar, his eyes sweeping over all of her. His gaze lingered on her shoes and he smiled, then his gaze stroked back up to her face again. "Mari, how long have you been awake?"

"Only a few minutes. Just long enough to hear you 'hmm' and 'uh-huh' a couple of times." She wrapped her arms around her waist, hugging the robe closed and making sure her tingling breasts didn't advertise her arousal. "If I may ask, who were you talking to so late?"

"Checking on our security and following up a lead on the baby."

She stood up straighter and joined him by the window, her heart hammering in her ears. "Did you find her family?"

"Sorry." He cupped her shoulder in a warm grasp, squeezing comfortingly. "Not yet. But we're working on it."

She forced herself to swallow and moisten her suddenly dry mouth. "Who is this 'we' you keep mentioning?"

"I'm a wealthy man now. Wealthy people have connections. I'm using them." His hand slid away, calluses snagging on her satin robe.

Calluses.

The thought of those fingers rasping along her skin made her shiver with want. God, she wasn't used to being this controlled by her body. She was a cerebral person, a thinker, a scientist. She needed to find level ground again, although it was a struggle.

Reining herself in, she eyed Rowan, assessing him. Her instincts told her he was holding something back about his conversation, but she couldn't decipher what that might be. She searched his face, really searched, and what a time to realize she'd never looked deeper than the surface of Rowan before. She'd known his history—a reformed bad boy, the saintly doctor saving the world and soaking up glory like a halo, while she was a person who preferred the shadows.

She'd only stepped into the spotlight now for the baby. And that made her wonder if his halo time had another purpose for him—using that notoriety for his causes. The possibility that she could have been mistaken about his ego, his swagger, gave her pause.

Of course she could just be seeking justification for how his kisses turned her inside out.

Then his hand slid down her arm until he linked fingers with her and tugged her toward the sofa. Her stomach leaped into her throat, but she didn't stop him, curious to see where this would lead. And reluctant to let go of his hand.

He sat, drawing her to sit beside him. Silently. Just staring back at her, his thumb stroking across the inside of her wrist.

Did he expect her to jump him? She'd already told him she wouldn't make the leap into bed with him. Had a part of her secretly hoped he would argue?

Still, he didn't speak or move.

She searched for something to say, anything to fill the empty space between them—and take her mind off the tantalizing feel of his callused thumb rubbing along her speeding pulse. "Do you really think Issa's family will be found?"

"I believe that every possible resource is being devoted to finding out who she is and where she came from."

The clean fresh scent of his aftershave rode every breath she took. She needed to focus on Issa first and foremost.

"Tomorrow—or rather, later this morning—we need to get serious about going public with the press. No more playing at dinner, pretend photos and controlled press releases. I need to use my notoriety to help her."

He squeezed her wrist lightly. "You don't have to put yourself in the line of fire so aggressively."

"Isn't that why you asked me to help you? To add oomph to the search?" His answer became too important to her.

"I could have handled the baby alone." He held her gaze, with undeniable truthfulness in his eyes. "If we're honest here, I wanted to spend more time with you."

Her tummy flipped and another of those tempting Rowan-scented breaths filled her. "You used the baby for selfish reasons? To get closer to me?"

"When you put it like that, it sounds so harsh."

"What *did* you mean then?"

He linked their fingers again, lifting their twined grasp and resting it against his chest. "Having you here does help with the baby's care and with finding the baby's family. But it also helps me get to know you better."

"Do you want to know me better or kiss me?"

His heart thudded against her hand as he leaned even closer, just shy of their lips touching. "Is there a problem with my wanting both?"

"You do understand that nothing is simple with me." Her breath mingled with his.

"Because of who you are? Yes, I realize exactly who you are."

And just that fast, reality iced over her. She could never forget who she was…her father's daughter. A princess. The next in the royal line since she had no siblings, no aunts or uncles. As much as she wanted to believe Rowan's interest in her was genuine, she'd been used and misunderstood too many times in the past.

She angled away from him. "I know you think I'm a spoiled princess."

"Sometimes we say things in anger that we don't mean. I apologize for that." He stretched his arm along the back of the sofa without touching her this time.

"What *do* you think of me?" The opinion of others hadn't mattered to her before…. Okay, that was a lie.

Her parents' opinion mattered. She'd cared what her first lover thought of her only to find he'd used her to get into her father's inner circle.

"Mari, I think you're smart and beautiful."

She grinned. "Organized and uptight."

He smiled back. "Productive, with restrained passions."

"I *am* a spoiled princess," she admitted, unable to resist the draw of his smile, wanting to believe what she saw in his eyes. "I've had every luxury, security, opportunity imaginable. I've had all the things this baby needs, things her mother is so desperate to give her she would give her away to a stranger. I feel awful and guilty for just wanting to be normal."

"Normal life?" He shook his head, the leather sofa creaking as he leaned back and away. "I had that so-called normal life and I still screwed up."

She'd read the press about him, the way he'd turned his life around after a drunk-driving accident as a teen. He was the poster boy for second chances, devoting his life to making amends.

Her negative reports on his program weren't always popular. Some cynics in the medical community had even suggested she had an ax to grind, insinuating he might have spurned her at some point. That assumption stung her pride more than a little.

Still, she couldn't deny the good he'd done with his clinic. The world needed more people like Dr. Rowan Boothe.

"You screwed up as a teenager, but you set yourself on the right path again once you went to that military high school."

"That doesn't erase my mistake. Nothing can." He plowed a hand through his hair. "It frustrates the hell out of me that the press wants to spin it into some kind of feel-good story. So yeah, I get your irritation with the whole media spin."

"But your story gives people hope that they can turn their lives around."

He mumbled a curse.

"What? Don't just go Grinchy on me." She tapped his elbow. "Talk. Like you did at dinner."

"Go Grinchy?" He cocked an eyebrow. "Is that really a word?"

"Of course it is. I loved that movie as a child. I watched a lot of Christmas movies flying across the ocean to spend Christmas with one parent or the other. So, back to the whole Grinchy face. What gives?"

"If you want to change my mood, then let's talk about something else." His arm slid from the back of the sofa until his hand cupped her shoulder. "What else did you enjoy about Christmas when you were a kid?"

"You're not going to distract me." With his words or his touch.

"Says who?" Subtly but deliberately, he pulled her closer.

And angled his mouth over hers.

Seven

Stunned still, Mari froze for an instant. Then all the simmering passion from her dream earlier came roaring to the surface. She looped her arms around Rowan's neck and inched closer to him on the sofa. The satin of her peignoir set made her glide across the leather smoother, easier, until she melted against him, opened her mouth and took him as boldly as he took her.

The sweep of his tongue carried the minty taste of toothpaste, the intoxicating warmth of pure him. His hands roved along her back, up and down her spine in a hypnotizing seduction. He teased his fingers up into her hair, massaging her scalp until her body relaxed, muscle by tense muscle, releasing tensions she hadn't even realized existed. Then he stirred a different sort of tension, a coiling of desire in her belly that pulled tighter and tighter until she arched against him.

Her breasts pressed to his chest, the hard wall of him

putting delicious pressure against her tender, oversensitized flesh.

He reclined with her onto the couch, tucking her beneath him with a possessive growl. She nipped his bottom lip and purred right back. The contrast of cool butter-soft leather beneath her and hot, hard male over her sent her senses on overload.

The feel of his muscled body stretching out over her, blanketing her, made her blood pulse faster, thicker, through her veins. She plucked at the leather string holding back his hair, pulled it loose and glory, glory, his hair slipped free around her fingers. She combed her hands through the coarse strands, just long enough to tickle her face as he kissed.

And this man sure did know how to kiss.

Not just with his mouth and his bold tongue, but he used his hands to stroke her, his body molding to hers. His knee slid between her legs. The thick pressure of his thigh against the core of her sent delicious shivers sparkling upward. All those sensations circled and tightened in her belly with a new intensity.

Her hands learned the planes and lines of him, along his broad shoulders, down his back to the firm butt she'd been checking out not too long ago. Every nerve ending tingled to life, urging her to take more—more of him and more of the moment.

She wanted all of him. Now.

Hooking a leg around his calf, she linked them, bringing him closer still. Her hips rocked against his, the thick length of his arousal pressing against her stomach with delicious promise of what they could have together. Soon. Although not soon enough. Urgency throbbed through her, pulsing into a delicious ache between her legs.

He swept aside her hair and kissed along the sensitive curve of her neck, nipping ever so lightly against her pulse. She hummed her approval and scratched gently over his back, along his shoulders, then down again to yank at his shirt. She couldn't get rid of their clothes fast enough. If she gave herself too long to think, too many practical reasons to stop would start marching through her mind—

A cool whoosh of air swept over her. She opened her eyes to see Rowan standing beside the sofa. Well, not standing exactly, but halfway bent over, his hands on his legs as he hauled in ragged breath after breath. His arousal was unmistakable, so why was he pulling away?

"What? Where?" She tried again to form a coherent sentence. "Where are you going?"

He stared at her in the moonlight, his chest rising and falling hard, like he'd run for miles. His expression was closed. His eyes inscrutable.

"Good night, Mariama."

Her brain couldn't make his words match up with what she was feeling. Something didn't add up. "Good night? That's it?"

"I need to stop now." He tucked his shirt in as he backed away. "Things are getting too intense."

She refused to acknowledge the twinge of hurt she felt at his words. She wasn't opening her emotions to this man.

"Yeah, I noticed." She brazened it out, still committed to re-creating the amazing feelings from her dream. "That intensity we were experiencing about twenty seconds ago was a good thing."

"It will be good, Mari. When you're ready."

Damn, but he confused her. She hated feeling like

the student in need of remedial help. The one who didn't "get" it.

"Um, hello, Rowan. I'm ready now."

"I just need for you to be sure." He backed away another step, his hair tousled from her hungry fingers. "See if you feel the same in the morning. Good night, Mariama."

He pivoted into his room and closed the door behind him.

Mari sagged back on the sofa, befuddled as hell. What was his game here? He bound her to him by enlisting her help with the baby. He clearly wanted her. Yet, he'd walked away.

She wasn't innocent. She'd been with men—two. The first was a one-night stand that had her clamping her legs shut for years to come after she'd learned he'd only wanted access to her family. Then one long-term deal with a man who'd been as introverted as her. Their relationship had dissolved for lack of attention, fading into nothing more than convenient sex. And then not so convenient. Still, the breakup had been messy, her former lover not taking well to having his ego stung over being dumped. He'd been a real jerk.

Whereas Rowan was being a total gentleman. Not pushing. Not taking advantage.

And he was driving her absolutely batty.

Holding back had threatened to drive Rowan over the edge all night long.

At least now he could move forward with the day. The salty morning breeze drifted through the open shutters as he tucked his polo shirt into his jeans, already anticipating seeing Mari. Soon. He'd never wanted a woman this much. Walking away from her last night had been almost impossible. But he was making progress. She wanted him and he needed this to be very, very reciprocal.

So he needed to move on with his plan to romance her. Neither of them had a presentation at the conference today. He suspected it wouldn't take much persuasion to convince her to skip out on sitting through boring slide presentations and rubber chicken.

During his sleepless night, he'd racked his brain for the best way to sweep her off her feet. She wasn't the most conventional of women. He'd decided to hedge his bets by going all out. He'd started off with the traditional stuff, a flower left on her pillow while she'd been in the shower. He'd also ordered her favorite breakfast delivered to her room. He planned to end the day with a beachside dinner and concert.

All traditional "dating" fare.

The afternoon's agenda, however, was a bit of a long shot. But then he figured it was best to hedge his bets with her. She'd seemed surprised by the breakfast, and he could have sworn she was at least a little charmed by his invitation to spend the day together. Although he still detected a hint of wariness.

But reminding her of how they could appease the press into leaving her alone by feeding them a story persuaded her. For now, at least. He just prayed the press conference went smoothly.

Rowan opened his bedroom door and found Mari already waiting for him in the sitting area with Issa cradled in her arms. She stood by the stroller, cooing to the baby and adjusting a pink bootie, her face softening with affection.

Mari wore a long silky sheath dress that glided across subtle curves as she swayed back and forth. And the pink tropical flower he'd left on her pillow was now tucked behind her ear. He stood captivated by her grace as she soothed the infant to sleep. Minutes—or maybe more—later, she leaned to place the baby in the stroller.

She glanced to the side, meeting his gaze with a smile. "Where are we going?"

Had she known he was there the whole time? Did she also know how damn difficult it had been to walk away from her last night? "It's a surprise."

"That makes me a little nervous." She straightened, gripping the stroller. "I'm not good at pulling off anything impetuous."

"We have a baby with us." He rested a hand on top of hers. "How dangerous could my plan be?"

Her pupils widened in response before her gaze skittered away. "Okay, fair enough." She pulled her hand from his and touched the exotic bloom tucked in her hair. "And thank you for the flower."

Ducking his head, he kissed her ear, right beside the flower, breathing in the heady perfume of her, even more tantalizing than the petals. "I'll be thinking of how you taste all day long."

He sketched a quick kiss along her regally high cheekbone before pulling back. Gesturing toward the private elevator, he followed her, taking in the swish of her curls spiraling just past her shoulders. What a time to realize how rarely he saw her with her hair down. She usually kept it pulled back in a reserved bun.

Except for last night when she'd gone to bed. And now.

It was all he could do to keep himself from walking up behind her, sliding his arms around her and pulling her flush against him. The thought of her bottom nestled against him, his face in the sweet curve of her neck… damn. He swallowed hard. Just damn.

He followed her into the elevator and thankfully the glide down went quickly, before he had too much time in the cubicle breathing in the scent of her. The elevator doors opened with a whoosh as hefty as his exhale.

His relief was short-lived. A pack of reporters waited just outside the resort entrance, ready for them to give their first official press conference. He'd expected it, of course. He'd even set this particular one up. But having Mari and the baby here put him on edge. Even knowing Elliot Starc's detail of bodyguards were strategically placed didn't give him total peace. He wondered what would.

Mari pushed the stroller while he palmed her back, guiding her through the lobby. Camera phones snap-snap-snapped as he ushered Mari and Issa across the marble floor. Gawkers whispered as they watched from beside towering columns and sprawling potted ferns.

The doorman waved them through the electric doors and out into chaos. Rowan felt Mari's spine stiffen. Protectiveness pumped through him anew.

He ducked his head toward her. "Are you sure you're okay with this? We can go back to the suite, dine on the balcony, spend our day off in a decadent haze of food and sunshine."

She shook her head tightly. "We proceed as planned. For Issa, I will do anything to get the word out about her story, whatever it takes to be sure she has a real family who loves her and appreciates what a gift she is."

Her ferocity couldn't be denied—and it stirred the hell out of him. Before he did something crazy like kiss her until they both couldn't think, he turned to the reporters gathered on the resort's stone steps.

"No questions today, just a statement," he said firmly with a smile. "Dr. Mandara and I have had our disagreements in the past, but we share a common goal in our desire…to help people in need. This is the holiday season and a defenseless child landed in our radar, this little girl. How could we look away? We're working together to care for this baby until her family can be found. If even Mari and I can work together, then maybe there's hope…."

He winked wryly and laughter rippled through the crowd.

Once they quieted, he continued, "That's all for now. We have a baby, a conference agenda and holiday shopping to juggle. Thank you and Merry Christmas, everyone."

Their bodyguards emerged from the crowd on cue and created a circular wall around them as they walked from the resort to the shopping strip.

Mari glanced up at him, her sandals slapping the wooden boardwalk leading to the stores and stalls of the shoreline marketplace. "Are we truly going shopping? I thought men hated shopping."

"It's better than hanging out inside eating conference food. I hope you don't mind. If you'd rather go back…"

"Bite your tongue." She hip-bumped him as he strode beside her.

"Onward then." He slipped his arm around her shoulders, tucking her to him as they walked.

She glanced up at him. "Thank you."

If he dipped his head, he could kiss her, but even though he'd set up this press coverage, he balked at that much exposure. "Thanks for what?"

"For the press conference, and taking the weight of that worry off me. You handled the media so perfectly.

I'm envious of your ease, though." She scrunched her elegant nose. "I wish I had that skill. Running from them hasn't worked out that well for me."

"I just hope the statement and all of those photos will help Issa."

"Why wouldn't it?"

Helping Interpol gain access to crooks around the world had given him insights into just how selfish, how Machiavellian, people could be. "Think of all the crackpots who will call claiming to know something just to attach themselves to a high-profile happening or hoping to gain access to you even for a short while knowing that DNA tests will later prove them to be frauds."

"God, I never thought of that," she gasped, her eyes wide and horrified.

He squeezed her shoulder reassuringly, all too aware of how perfectly she fit to his side. "The police are going to be busy sifting through the false leads that come through."

"That's why you wanted to wait a day to officially announce we're fostering her...." she whispered softly to herself as they passed a cluster of street carolers.

"Why did you think I waited?" He saw a whisper of chagrin shimmer in her golden eyes. "Did you think I was buying time to hit on you?"

She lifted a dark eyebrow. "Were you?"

"Maybe." Definitely.

She looked away, sighing. "Honestly, I'm not sure what I thought. Since I stumbled into your suite with that room-service cart, things have been...crazy. I've barely had time to think, things are happening so fast. I just hate to believe anyone would take advantage of this precious baby's situation for attention or reward money."

The reality of just how far people would go made his

jaw flex. "We'll wade through them. No one gains access to this child or you until they've been completely vetted. We will weed through the false claims and selfish agendas. Meanwhile, she's safe with us. She turns toward your voice already."

"You're nice to say that, but she's probably just in search of her next bottle."

"Believe what you want. I know differently." He'd seen scores of mothers and children file through his clinic—biological and adoptive. Bonds formed with or without a blood connection.

"Are you arguing with me? I thought we were supposed to be getting along now. Isn't that what you said at the press conference?"

"I'm teasing you. Flirting. There's a difference." Unable to resist, he pressed a kiss to her forehead.

"Oh."

"Relax. I'm not going to hit on you here." There were far too many cameras for him to be too overt. "Although a longer kiss would certainly give the press something to go wild about. Feed them tidbits and they'll quit digging for other items."

Furrows dug into her forehead. "But it feels too much like letting them win."

"I consider it controlling the PR rather than letting it control me." He guided her by her shoulders, turning toward a reporter with a smile before walking on. "Think about all the positive publicity you're racking up for your father."

"This may have started out to be about keeping the press off my back, but now it's more about the baby."

He agreed with her on that account. But the worry on her face reminded him to stay on track with his plan.

"This conversation is getting entirely too serious for a day of fun and relaxation."

"Of course..." She swiped her hand over her forehead, squeezing her eyes closed for an instant before opening them again and smiling. "Who are you shopping for today? For your family?"

"In a sense."

He stopped in front of a toy store.

Her grin widened, her kissable lips glistening with a hint of gloss. "Are we shopping for Issa?"

"For the kids at my clinic."

Toy shopping with Rowan and Issa, like they were a family, tore at Mari's heart throughout the day. The man who'd left a flower on her pillow and chosen her favorite breakfast was charming. But the man who went shopping for the little patients at his free clinic?

That man was damn near irresistible.

Riding the elevator back up to their suite, she grabbed the brass bar for balance. Her unsteady feet had nothing to do with exhaustion or the jerk of the elevator— and everything to do with the man standing beside her.

Her mind swirled with memories of their utterly carefree day. The outing had been everything she could have hoped for and more. Sure, the paparazzi had followed them, lurking, but Rowan had controlled them, fielding their questions while feeding them enough tidbits to keep them from working themselves into a frenzy. Best of all, Issa had gotten her press coverage. Hopefully the right people would see it.

As much as Mari's stomach clenched at the thought of saying goodbye to the baby, she wanted what was best for the child. She wanted Issa to feel—and be— loved unreservedly. Every child deserved that. And

Rowan was doing everything possible to help this child he'd never met, just like he did the patients at his clinic, even down to the smallest detail.

Such as their shopping spree.

It would have been easier to write it off as a show for the press or a trick to win her over. But he had a list of children's names with notes beside them. Not that she could read his stereotypically wretched doctor's scrawl. But from the way he consulted the list and made choices, he'd clearly made a list of kids' names and preferences. The bodyguards had been kept busy stowing packages in the back of a limo trailing them from store to store.

And he hadn't left Issa off his list. The baby now had a new toy in her stroller, a plush zebra, the black-and-white stripes captivating the infant. The vendor had stitched the baby's name in pink on the toy.

Issa.

The one part of her prior life the little one carried with her—a name. Used for both boys and girls, meaning savior. Appropriate this time of year... Her feet kicked. Could the name be too coincidental? Could whoever left the baby have made up the name to go with the season—while leading authorities astray?

She leaned in to stroke the baby's impossibly soft cheek. Issa's lashes swept open and she stared up at Mari for a frozen moment, wide dark eyes looking up with such complete trust Mari melted. What happened if family came forward and they didn't love her as she deserved?

Those thoughts threatened to steal Mari's joy and she shoved them aside as the elevator doors whooshed open. She refused to let anything rob her of this per-

fect day and the promise of more. More time with Issa.
More time with Rowan.

More kisses?

More of everything?

He'd walked away last night because he thought she
wasn't ready. Maybe he was right. Although the fact
that he cared about her needs, her well-being, made it
all the more difficult to keep him at arm's length. And
she couldn't even begin to imagine how his plans for
seducing her fit into this whole charade with the baby.

Questions churned in her mind, threatening to steal
the joy from the day. In a rare impulsive move, she decided to simply go with the flow. She would quit worrying about when or if they would sleep together and
just enjoy being with Rowan. Enjoy the flirting.

Revel in the chemistry they shared rather than wearing herself out denying its existence.

Butterflies stirred in her stomach. She pushed the
stroller into their suite just as Rowan's arm shot out to
stop her.

"Someone's here," he warned a second before a
woman shot up from the sofa.

A woman?

The butterflies slowed and something cold settled
in her stomach. Dread?

A redhead with a freckled nose and chic clothes
squealed, "Rowan!"

The farm-fresh bombshell sprinted across the room
and wrapped her arms around Rowan's neck.

Dread quickly shifted to something darker.

Jealousy.

Eight

Rowan braced his feet as the auburn-haired whirl-wind hit him full force. He'd spoken with his business partner and the partner's wife, Hillary, about the current situation. But he'd assured them Elliot Starc had things under control. Apparently his friends weren't taking him at his word.

Who else was waiting in the suite to blindside him? So much for romance tonight.

"Hillary." Rowan hugged his friend fast before pulling away. "Not that I'm unhappy to see you, but what are you doing here tonight?"

She patted his face. "You should know that word spreads fast among the Brotherhood and everyone available is eager to help." She glanced over her shoulder at Mari and the baby. "And of course, we're insanely curious about your new situation."

Mari looked back and forth between them, a look of confusion on her face. "The Brotherhood?"

"A nickname for some of my high school class-mates," Rowan explained. "We used to call ourselves the Alpha Brotherhood."

They still did, actually, after a few drinks over a game of cards. The name had started as a joke between them, a way of thumbing their noses at the frat-boy types, and after a while, the label stuck.

Hillary thrust a hand toward Mari. "Hi, I'm Hillary Donavan. I'm married to Rowan's former classmate and present business partner, Troy."

Mari's eyebrows arched upward. "Oh, your husband is the computer mogul."

Hillary took over pushing the stroller and preceded them into the suite as if it was her hotel penthouse. "You can go ahead and say it. My husband is the Robin Hood Hacker."

"I wasn't..." Mari stuttered, following the baby buggy deeper into the room. "I wouldn't...uh..."

"It's okay," Hillary said with a calm smile that had smoothed awkward moments in her days as an event planner for high-powered D.C. gatherings. "You can relax. Everyone knows my husband's history."

Mari smiled apologetically, leaning into the stroller to pull the sleeping baby out and cradle her protectively in her arms. "I'm not particularly good with chitchat."

"That's all right. I talk plenty for two people." She cupped the back of the infant's head. "What an ador-able baby. Issa, right?"

"Yes." Rowan pushed the stroller to a corner, light-weight gauzy pink blanket trailing out the side. "Did you see the gossip rags or did the Brotherhood tell you that, too?"

Hillary made herself at home on the leather sofa. "Actually, I'm here to help. Troy and Rowan are more than just business partners on that computer diagnostics project you so disapprove of—" Hillary winked to take the sting out the dig "—they're also longtime friends. I have some last-minute Christmas shopping to do for those tough-to-buy-for people in my life, and voilà. Coming here seemed the perfect thing to do."

The pieces came together in Rowan's mind, Hillary's appearance now making perfect sense. While the Brotherhood kept their Interpol work under wraps, Hillary knew about her husband's freelance agent work and Salvatore had even taken her into the fold for occasional missions. Now she was here. He should have thought of it himself, if his brain hadn't been scrambled by a certain sexy research scientist.

Hillary would make the perfect bodyguard for Mari and Issa. No one would question her presence and she added a layer of protection to this high-profile situation.

Although sometimes the whole Interpol connection also came with dangers. God, he was in the middle of an impossible juggling act.

The baby started fussing and Rowan extended his arms to take her. Mari hesitated, tucking the baby closer. Rowan lifted an eyebrow in surprise.

"Mari? I can take her." He lifted the baby from Mari's arms. "You two keep talking."

"Wow." Hillary laughed. "You sure handle that tiny tyke well. No wonder you're dubbed one of the world's hottest bachelors. Snap a photo of you now and you'll need your own bodyguard."

Mari's smile went tight and Rowan wondered... Holy hell, she couldn't be jealous. Could she? Was that the same look he'd seen drifting through her eyes when Hillary had hugged him earlier? He wanted her to desire him, but he also wanted—needed—for her to trust him.

"Enough, Hillary. You were talking about Troy's computer search...."

"Right—" she turned back to Mari "—and you're taking care of the baby, Rowan. So vamoose. Go fill out your list for Santa. I've got this."

Rowan cocked an eyebrow over being so summarily dismissed. And putting Issa in the bassinet in another room would give him the perfect excuse to slip away and call Troy.

Not to mention time to regroup for the next phase of winning over Mari. He'd made progress with her today.

Now he just had to figure out how to persuade his friends to give him enough space to take that romancing to the next level.

Mari sank to the edge of the sofa. Her head was spinning at how fast things were changing around her. Not to mention how fast this woman was talking.

"Hold on a moment, please." Mari raised a hand. "What were you saying about computer searches into Issa's past?"

Hillary dropped into the wide rattan chair beside her. "No worries. It's all totally legal computer work. I promise. Troy walks on the right side of the law these days. And yes, it's okay to talk about it. I know about my husband's past, and I assume you know about Rowan's. But they've both changed. They're genuinely trying to make amends in more ways than most could imagine."

Mari blinked in the wake of Hurricane Hillary, confused. Why would Rowan have needed to make amends for anything? Sure, he'd led a troubled life as a teen, but his entire adult life had been a walking advertisement for charity work. Even if she disputed some of his methods, she couldn't deny his philanthropic spirit. "I've read the stories of his good deeds."

"There's so much more to Rowan than those stories."

She knew that already. The press adored him and his work, and she had to admit his clinic had helped many. She just wished they could come to an agreement on how to make his work—the computerized side and even the personal side—more effective. If she could solve that problem, who knew how many more small clinics in stretched-thin outposts of the world would benefit from Rowan's model of aid?

"Hillary, why are you telling me this?"

"The competitive animosity between the two of you is not a secret." She tipped her head to the side, twirling a strand of red hair contemplatively. "So I find it strange that you're here."

"I'm here for the baby."

"Really?" Hillary crossed her legs, her eyes glimmering with humor and skepticism. No getting anything past this woman. "There are a million ways the two of you could care for this child other than sharing a suite."

Mari bristled, already feeling overwhelmed by this confident whirlwind who looked like a Ralph Lauren model in skinny jeans and a poet's shirt.

Smoothing her hands over her sack dress, Mari sat up stiffly, channeling every regal cell in her body. "This is quite a personal conversation to be having with someone I only just met."

"You're right. I apologize if I've overstepped." She held up a hand, diamond wedding band set winking in the sunlight. "I've become much more extroverted since marrying Troy. I just wanted you to know Rowan's a better man than people think. A better man than he knows."

Great. Someone else pointing out the perfection of Dr. Rowan Boothe. As if Mari didn't already know. God, how she resented the feelings of insecurity pumping through her. She wanted to be the siren in the peignoir, the confident woman certain that Rowan wanted her with every fiber of his soul. And yes, she knew that was melodramatic and totally unscientific.

Forcing her thoughts to slow and line up logically, she realized that Rowan's eyes had followed her all day long—no skinny jeans needed. And Hillary was right. He and Mari both could have figured out a dozen different ways to care for this baby and stir publicity without sharing a suite. She was here because she wanted to be and Rowan wanted her here, as well.

No more flirting. No more games. No more holding back. She burned to sleep with Rowan.

The next time she had him alone, she intended to see the seduction through to its full, satisfying conclusion.

Finally, Rowan closed his suite door after dinner with Hillary, Troy and Elliot. He plowed his hands through his hair as Mari settled the baby for the night in his room.

He appreciated the help of his friends—but by the end of supper he had never been happier to see them all head to their own suites. Troy and Hillary were staying in the suite across the hall. Elliot Starc was a floor below, monitoring the surveillance vans outside the resort.

Rowan was more than a little surprised that his friends felt such a need to rally around him just because another orphan had landed on his doorstep. Issa wasn't the first—and she certainly wouldn't be the last—child in need of his patronage.

He suspected his friends' increased interest had something to do with Mari's involvement. No doubt he hadn't been as successful as he would have liked at hiding his attraction to her all these years. They were here out of curiosity as well as genuine caring, stepping up on a personal level, even if Mari didn't know the full weight of what they brought to the table for security and he wasn't in a position to tell her.

Now that a story had broken about an orphan at Christmastime, the attention was swelling by the second. Holiday mayhem made it tougher than ever to record all the comings and goings at the resort. Bogus leads were also coming in by the hundreds. So far no sign of a valid tip. Hillary and Troy were rechecking the police work through computer traces, using Interpol databases.

Intellectually, he understood these things took time and persistence, but thinking about the kid's future, worrying about her, made this more personal than analytical.

Somewhere out there, the baby's family had to be seeing the news reports. Even if they didn't want to claim her, surely someone would step forward with information. Even if the answer came in the form of official surrender of parental rights, at least they would know.

He understood full well how family ties didn't always turn out to be as ideal as one would hope. Memories of his brother's death, of his parents' grief and denial burned through him. He charged across the sitting area to the bar. He started to reach for the scotch and stopped himself. After the way his brother died...

Hell, no.

He opted for a mug of fresh local ginger tea and

one of the Christmas sugar cookies instead and leaned against the bar, staring out over the water as he bit the frosted tree cookie in half. Tomorrow, he and Mari both had conference presentations, then this weekend, the closing dinner and ball. Time was ticking away for all of them. He had to make the most of every moment. Tomorrow, he'd arranged for a spa appointment for Mari after her last presentation. Surely she would appreciate some privacy after all the scrutiny....

The door from Rowan's room opened. Mari slid through and closed it quietly after her. "Baby's sleeping soundly. I would have taken her tonight, you know."

"Fair is fair," he said. "We struck a bargain."

"You're a stubborn man. But then I understand that trait well."

Walking toward him, her silvery-gray sheath dress gliding over her sleek figure, she set the nursery monitor on the edge of the bar. Christmas tunes played softly over the airwaves—jazz versions, soft and soothing. Mari had fallen into the habit of setting her iPhone beside the monitor and using the music to reassure herself the listening device was still on.

She poured herself a mug of steaming ginger tea as well, adding milk and honey. Cupping the thick pottery in both hands, she drank half then cradled the mug to her with a sigh.

He skimmed his knuckles along her patrician cheekbones. "Are you okay?"

Nodding, she set aside her glass. "I just didn't expect the press coverage to be so...comprehensive."

Was it his imagination or did she lean into his touch.

"You're a princess. What you do makes the news." Although even he was surprised at just how intense the media attention had become.

The hotel staff had closed off access to their floor aside from them and the Donavans, a measure taken after a reporter was injured on a window-washing unit trying to get a bonus photo. Rowan rubbed at a kink in the back of his neck, stress-induced from worrying his tail off about all the possible holes in the security. He wasn't sure he felt comfortable taking Mari and Issa out of the hotel again, even with guards.

"But I wanted to bring positive coverage for Issa. Not all of these cranks..."

And she didn't know the half of it. Troy had informed him about a handful of the more colorful leads the police hadn't bothered mentioning. A woman claiming to be Mari's illegitimate half sister had called to say the baby belonged to her. Another call had come from an area prison with someone saying their infant daughter resembled Issa and she thought it was her twin, whom they'd thought died at birth.

All of which turned out to be false, but there was no need to make Mari more upset by sharing the details. "My contacts will sift through them."

"Who are these contacts you keep talking about? Like Hillary and her husband?" She picked up the glass again and sipped carefully.

His glass.

His body tightened as her lips pressed to the edge.

He cleared his throat. "I went to a military high school. Makes sense that some of them would end up in law enforcement positions."

"It was a military *reform* school." She eyed him over the rim of the tumbler through long lashes.

"Actually, about half were there because they wanted a future in the military or law enforcement." He rattled off the details, anything to keep from thinking about how badly he wanted to take that glass from her and kiss her until they both forgot about talking and press conferences. "The rest of us were there because we got into trouble."

"Your Alpha Brotherhood group—you trust these friends with Issa's future?"

"Implicitly."

Shaking her head, she looked away. "I wish I could be as sure about whom to trust."

"You're worried."

"Of course."

"Because you care." Visions of her caring for the baby, insisting Issa stay in her room tonight even though it was his turn, taunted him with how attached she was becoming to the little one already. There was so much more to this woman than he'd known or guessed. She was more emotional than she'd ever let on. Which brought him back to the strange notion that she'd been jealous of Hillary.

A notion he needed to dispel. "What did you think of Hillary?"

"She's outspoken and she's a huge fan of yours." She folded her arms over her chest.

"You can't be jealous."

"At first, when she hugged you…I wondered if she was a girlfriend," she admitted. "Then I realized it might not be my right to ask."

"I kissed you. You have a right to question." He met her gaze full-on, no games or hidden agendas. Just pure honesty. "For the record, I'm the monogamous type. When I'm with a woman, I'm sure as hell not kissing other women."

Her eyes flashed with quick relief before she tipped

her head to the side and touched his chest lightly. "What happened last night—"

"What almost happened—"

"Okay, almost happened, along with the parts that did—"

"I understand." He pressed a hand over hers, wanting to reassure her before she had a chance to start second-guessing things and bolting away. "You want to say it can't happen. Not again."

"Hmm…" She frowned, toying with the simple watch on her wrist. "Have you added mind reader to your list of accomplishments now? If so, please do tell me why I would insist on pushing you away."

"Because we have to take care of the baby." He folded her hand in his and kissed her knuckles, then her wrist. "Your devotion to her is a beautiful thing."

"That's a lovely compliment. Thank you. I would say the same about you."

"A compliment?" he bantered back. "I did *not* expect that."

"Why ever not?" She stepped closer until her breasts almost brushed his chest.

The unmistakably seductive move wasn't lost on him. His pulse kicked up a notch as he wondered just how far she would take this.

And how far he should let it go.

"There is the fact that you haven't missed an opportunity to make it clear how much you don't like me or my work."

"That could be a compelling reason to keep my distance from you." She placed her other hand on his chest, tipping her face up to him until their lips were a whisper apart.

"Be on notice…" He took in the deep amber of her

eyes, the flush spreading across her latte-colored, creamy skin. "I plan to romance you, sweep you off your feet even."

"You are—" she paused, leaning into him, returning his intense gaze "—a confusing man. I thought I knew you but now I'm finding I don't understand you at all. But you need to realize that after last night's kiss…"

"It was more than a kiss," he said hoarsely.

"You're absolutely right on that." Her fingers crawled up his chest until she tapped his bottom lip.

He captured her wrist again just over the thin watch. He thought of the bracelets he'd surreptitiously picked up for her at the marketplace, looking forward to the right moment to give them to her. "But I will not make love to you until you ask me. You have to know that."

"You're mighty confident." Her breath carried heat and a hint of the ginger tea.

Who knew tea could be far more intoxicating than any liquor? "Hopeful."

"Good." Her lips moved against his. "Because I'm asking."

And damn straight he didn't intend to walk away from her again.

Nine

Mari arched up onto her toes to meet Rowan's mouth sealing over hers. Pure want flooded through her. Each minute had felt like an hour from the moment she'd decided to act on her desire tonight until the second he'd kissed her.

Finally, she would be with him, see this crazy attraction through. Whether they were arguing or working together, the tension crackled between them. She recognized that now. They'd been moving toward this moment for years.

She nipped his bottom lip. "We have to be quiet so we don't wake the baby."

"Hmm…" His growl rumbled his chest against her. "Sounds challenging."

"Just how challenging can we make it?" She grazed her nails down his back, the fabric of his shirt carrying the warmth and scent of him.

"Is that a dare?"

She tucked her hands into the back pockets of his jeans as she'd dreamed of doing more than once. "Most definitely."

Angling his head to the side, he stared into her eyes. "And you're sure you're ready for this?"

She dug her fingers into his amazing tush. "Could you quit being so damn admirable? I'm very clearly propositioning you. I am an adult, a very smart adult, totally sober, and completely turned on by you. If that's not clear enough for you, then how about this? Take me to bed or to the couch, but take me now."

A slow and sexy smile creased dimples into his sun-bronzed face. "How convenient you feel that way since you absolutely mesmerize me."

Her stomach fluttered at the obvious appreciation in his eyes, his voice. His *touch.* He made her feel like the sensuous woman who wore peignoirs. He made her feel sexy. Sexier than any man ever had, and yes, that was a part of his appeal.

But she couldn't deny she'd always found him attractive. Who wouldn't? He took handsome to a whole new level, in a totally unselfconscious way. The blond streaks in his hair came from the sun—his muscles from hard work.

And those magnificent callused hands... She could lose herself in the pure sensation of his caress.

He inched aside the strap of her silvery-gray dress. She'd chosen the silky fabric for the decadent glide along her skin—yes, she usually preferred shapeless clothes, but the appreciation in Rowan's eyes relayed loud and clear he'd never judged her by what she wore. He saw her. The woman. And he wanted her.

That knowledge sent a fresh thrill up her spine.

He kissed along her bared neck, to her shoulder, his teeth lightly snapping her champagne-colored satin bra strap—another of her hidden decadences, beautiful underwear. Her head fell back, giving him fuller access. But she didn't intend to be passive in this encounter. Not by a long shot. Her hands soaked up the play of his muscles flexing in his arms as she stroked down, down, farther still to his waistband.

She tugged his polo shirt free and her fingers crawled up under the warm cotton to find even hotter skin. She palmed his back, scaled the hard planes of his shoulder blades as a jazz rendering of "The First Noel" piped through the satellite radio. He was her latest fantasies come to life.

Unable to wait a second longer, she yanked the shirt over his head even if that meant he had to draw his mouth away from her neck. She flung aside his polo, the red shirt floating to rest on the leather sofa. Fire heated his eyes to the hottest blue flame. He skimmed off the other strap of her dress until the silk slithered down her body, hooking briefly on her hips before she shimmied it the rest of the way off to pool at her feet. She kicked aside her sandals as she stepped out of the dress.

His gaze swept over her as fully as she took in the bared expanse of his broad chest, the swirls of hair, the sun-bronzed skin. He traced down the strap of her bra, along the lace edging the cups of her bra, slowly, deliberately outlining each breast. Her nipples beaded against the satin, tight and needy. She burned to be closer to him, as close as possible.

Her breath hitched in her throat and she stepped into his arms. The heat of his skin seared her as if he'd stored up the African sun inside him and shared it with her now.

"Here," she insisted, "on the sofa or the floor. I don't care. Just hurry."

"Princess, I have waited too damn long to rush this. I intend to have you completely and fully, in a real bed. I would prefer it was my bed, but there's a baby snoozing in the bassinet in my room. So let's go to yours."

"Fine," she agreed frantically. "Anywhere, the sooner the better." She slipped a finger into the waistband of his jeans and tugged.

"I like a lady who knows what she wants. Hell, I just like you."

His hands went to the front clasp of her bra and plucked it open and away with deft hands. She gasped as the overhead fan swooshed air over her bared flesh. Then he palmed both curves, warming her with a heat that spread into a tingling fire.

Through the haze of passion she realized her hand was still on his buckle. She fumbled with his belt, then the snap of his jeans, his zipper, until she found his arousal hard and straining against her hand. A growl rumbled low in his throat and she reveled in the sound. Drew in the scent of his soap and his sweat, perspiration already beading his brow from his restraint as she learned the feel of him. She stroked the steely length down, up and again.

"We have to be quiet," she reminded him.

"Both of us," he said with a promise in his voice and in his narrowed eyes.

One of his hands slid from her breast down to her panties, dipping inside, gliding between her legs. She was moist and ready for him. If she'd had her way they would be naked and together on the sofa. He was the one who'd insisted on drawing this out, but then they'd always been competitive.

Although right now that competition was delivering a tense and delicious result rather than the frustration of the past. She bit her bottom lip to hold back a whimper of pleasure. He slipped two fingers inside, deeper, stroking and coaxing her into a moist readiness. She gripped his shoulders, her fingernails digging half-moons into his tanned skin. Each glide took her higher until her legs went weak and he locked an arm around her back.

She gasped against his neck, so close to fulfillment. Aching for completion. "Let's take this to the bed."

"Soon, I promise." His late-day beard rasped against her cheek and he whispered in her ear, "But first, I need to protect you."

She gritted her teeth in frustration over the delay. "Rowan, there are guards stationed inside and outside of the hotel. Can we talk about security forces later?"

Cupping her face in his broad palms, he kissed the tip of her nose. "I mean I need to get birth control."

"Oh…" She gasped, surprised that she hadn't thought of it herself. She'd come in here with the intention of seducing him and she hadn't given a thought to the most important element of that union. So much for her genius IQ in the heat of the moment.

"I'll take care of it." He stepped away and disappeared from her room, his jeans slung low on his hips. Lean muscles rippled with every step.

She was an intelligent, modern woman. A scientist. A woman of logic. She liked to believe she would have realized before it was too late…. Before she could complete the thought, Rowan returned. He tossed a box of condoms on the bed.

"My goodness," she said, smiling, "you're an ambitious man."

"I'll take that as another challenge."

"Sounds like one where we're both winners. Now how about getting rid of those jeans."

"Your wish is my command, Princess." He toed off his shoes, no socks on, and peeled down his jeans without once taking his eyes off her.

His erection strained against his boxers and she opened her arms for him to join her. Then he was kissing her again and, oh, my, but that man knew how to kiss. The intensity of him, the way he was so completely focused on her and the moment fulfilled a long-ignored need to be first with a man. How amazing that the man who would view her this way—see only her—would be Rowan.

He reclined with her on the bed, into the thick comforter and stack of tapestry pillows, the crash and recede of the waves outside echoing the throb of her pulse. The sound of the shore, the luxurious suite, the hard-bodied man stretched over her was like a fantasy come true.

Only one thing kept it from being complete—something easily taken care of. She hooked her thumbs into the band of his boxers and inched them down. He smiled against her mouth as his underwear landed on the floor. Finally—thank heavens—finally, they met bare body to bare body, flesh-to-flesh. The rigid length of him pressed against her stomach, heating her with the promise of pleasure to come.

She dragged her foot up the back of his calf, hooking her leg around him, rocking her hips against him. He shifted his attention from her lips to her neck, licking along her collarbone before reaching her breasts—his mouth on one, his hand on the other. He touched and tasted her with an intuition for what she craved and more, finding nuances of sensitive patches of skin she hadn't realized were favored spots.

And she wanted to give him the same bliss.

Her fingers slid between them until her hand found his erection, exploring the length and feel of him. His forehead fell to rest against her collarbone. His husky growl puffed along oversensitized skin as she continued to stroke. Her thumb glided along the tip, smoothing a damp pearl, slickening her caress. Her mind filled with images of all the ways she wanted to love him through the night, with her hands and her mouth, here and in the shower. She whispered those fantasies in his ear and he throbbed in response in her hand.

Groaning, he reached out to snatch up the box of condoms. Rolling to his side, he clasped her wrist and moved her hand away, then sheathed himself. She watched, vowing next time she would do that for him.

Next time? Definitely a next time. And a next night.

Already she was thinking into the future and that was a scary proposition. Better to live in the now and savor this incredible moment. She clasped Rowan's shoulders as he shifted back over her again.

He balanced on his elbows, holding his weight off her. The thick pressure of him between her legs had her wriggling to get closer, draw him in deeper. She swept her other leg up until her ankles hooked around his waist. Her world filled with the sight of his handsome face and broad shoulders blocking out the rest of the world.

He hooked a hand behind her knee. "Your legs drive me crazy. Do you know that?"

"I do now. I also know you're driving me crazy waiting. I want all of you. Now." She dug her heels into his buttocks and urged him to…

Fill her.

Stretch her.

Thrill her.

Her back bowed up to meet him thrust for thrust, hushed sigh for sigh. Perspiration sealed them together, cool sheets slipping and bunching under them. In a smooth sweep, he kicked the comforter and tapestry pillows to the floor.

Tension gathered inside her, tightening in her belly. Her head dug back into the mattress, the scent of them mingling and filling every gasping breath. He touched her with reverence and perception, but she didn't want gentle or reverent. She needed edgy; she needed completion.

She pushed at his shoulder and flipped him to his back, straddling him, taking him faster and harder, his heated gaze and smile of approval all the encouragement she needed. His hands sketched up her stomach to her breasts, circling and plucking at her nipples as she came, intensifying waves of pleasure, harder, straight to the core of her. She rode the sensations, rode him, taking them both to the edge…and into a climax. Mutual. She bit her bottom lip to hold back the sounds swelling inside her as she stayed true to their vow to keep quiet. Rowan's jaw flexed, his groans mingling with her sighs.

Each rolling wave of bliss drew her, pulling her into a whirlpool of total muscle-melting satisfaction. Her arms gave way and she floated to rest on top of him. Rowan's chest pumped beneath her with labored breaths. His arms locked around her, anchoring her to him and to the moment.

Her body trembled in the wake of each aftershock rippling through her.

Exhaustion pulled at her but she knew if she slept, morning would come too fast with too many questions and possibilities that could take this away. So she blinked back sleep, focusing on multicolored lights beyond the window. Yachts, a sailboat, a ferry. She took in the details to stay awake so once her languid body regained strength, she could play out all those fantasies with Rowan.

She wanted everything she could wring from this stolen moment in case this night was all they could have before she retreated to the safety and order of her cold, clinical world.

"Are you asleep?" Mari's soft voice whispered through Rowan's haze as he sprawled beside her.

He'd wanted Mari for years. He'd known they would be good together. But no way in hell could he have predicted just how mind-blowingly incredible making love to this woman would be.

Sleep wasn't even an option with every fiber of him saturated with the satiny feel of her, the floral scent of her, the driving need to have her again and again until…

His mind stopped short of thoughts of the end. "I'm awake. Do you need something?"

Was she about to boot him out of her bed? Out of her life? He knew too well how fast the loyalties of even good people could shift. He grabbed the rumpled sheet free from around his feet and whipped it out until it fanned to rest over them.

She rolled toward him, her fingers toying with the hair on his chest. "I'm good. *This* is good, staying right here, like this. The past couple of days have been so frenzied, it's a relief to be in the moment."

"I hear ya." He kissed the top of her head, thinking of the bracelets he'd bought for her from the market and planning the right time to place them on her elegant arm.

Her fingers slowed and she looked up at him through long sweeping eyelashes. "You're very good with Issa. Have you ever thought about having kids of your own?"

His voice froze in his throat for a second. He'd given up on perfect family life a long time ago when he'd woken in the hospital to learn he and his brother were responsible for a woman losing her baby. Any hope of resurrecting those dreams died the day his brother crashed his truck into the side of a house.

Rowan sketched his fingers along Mari's stomach. He'd built a new kind of family with the Brotherhood and his patients. "I have my kids at the clinic, children that need me and depend on me."

"So you know that it's possible to love children that aren't your blood relation."

Where was she going with this? And then holy hell, it became all too clear. She was thinking about the possibility of keeping Issa beyond this week. "Are you saying that you're becoming attached to the little rug rat?"

"How could I not?" She leaned over him, resting her chin on her folded hands as she looked into his eyes. "I wonder if Issa landed with me for a reason. I've always planned not to get married. I thought that meant no kids for me—I never considered myself very good with them. But with Issa, I know what to do. She even responds to my voice already."

She was right about that. They shared a special bond that had to be reassuring to an infant whose world had been turned upside down by abandonment. But questions about the baby's past *would* be answered soon. He thought of Hillary and Troy working their tails off to find the baby's family. He hated to think of Mari setting herself up for heartache.

She shook her head before he could think of how

to remind her. "I know it's only been a couple of days and she could well have family out there who wants her. Or her mother might change her mind. I just hate the limbo."

He swept her hair from her face and kissed her, hard. "You won't be in limbo for long, I can promise you that." Guilt pinched over how he'd brought her into this, all but forced her to stay with him. "My friends and I won't rest until we find the truth about Issa's past. That's a good thing, you know."

"Of course I do. Let's change the subject." She pulled a wobbly smile. "I think it's amazing the way your friends all came to help you at the drop of a hat."

"It's what we do for each other." Just as he'd done his best to help his buddy Conrad reconcile with his wife earlier this year. He owed Conrad for helping him start the clinic, but he would have helped regardless.

"In spite of your rocky teenage years, you and your friends have all turned into incredible success stories. I may not always agree with some of your projects, but your philanthropic work is undeniable. It's no secret that your other friend, the casino owner—Conrad Hughes— has poured a lot of money into your clinic, as well."

He tensed at her mention of one of his Alpha Brotherhood buddies, wishing he could share more about the other side of his life. Needing to warn her, to ensure she didn't get too close. There weren't many women who could live with the double life he and his friends led with their Interpol work. Mari had enough complicating her life with her heritage. Better to keep the conversation on well-known facts and off anything that could lead to speculation.

"Conrad invested the start-up cash for my clinic. He

deserves the credit. My financial good fortune came later."

"No need to be so modest. Even before your invention of the diagnostics program, you could have had a lucrative practice anywhere and you chose to be here in Africa, earning a fraction of the salary."

He grunted, tunneling his hand under the sheet to cup her butt and hopefully distract her. "I got by then and I get by even better now."

She smiled against his chest. "Right, the billions you made off that diagnostics program we keep arguing about. I could help you make it better."

He smacked her bottom lightly. "Is that really what you want to talk about and risk a heated debate?"

"Why are you so quick to deflect accolades? The press is totally in love with you. You could really spin that, if you wanted."

He grimaced. "No, thanks."

She elbowed up on his chest. "I do understand your reticence. But think about it. You could inspire other kids. Sure you went to a military reform school, but you studied your butt off for scholarships to become a doctor, made a fortune and seem to be doing your level best to give it all away."

"I'm not giving it *all* away," he said gruffly, a sick feeling churning in his gut at the detour this conversation was taking. He avoided that damn press corps for just this reason. He didn't want anyone digging too deeply and he sure as hell didn't want credit for some noble character he didn't possess. "If I donate everything, I'll be broke and no good to anyone. I'm investing wisely."

"While donating heavily of your money and time."

Throwing all his resources into the black hole of guilt

that he'd never fill. Ever. He took a deep breath to keep that dark cavern at bay.

"Stop, okay?" He kissed her to halt her words. "I do what I do because it's the right thing. I have to give back, to make up for my mistakes."

Her forehead furrowed. "For your drunk-driving accident in high school? I would say you've more than made restitution. You could hire other doctors to help you carry the load."

"How can a person ever make restitution for lives lost?" he barked out, more sharply than he'd intended. But now that he'd started, there was no going back. "Do you know why I was sentenced to the military reform school for my last two years of high school?"

"Because you got in a drunk-driving accident and a woman was injured. You made a horrible, horrible mistake, Rowan. No one's denying that. But it's clear to anyone looking that you've turned your life around."

"You've done your homework where my diagnostics model is concerned, but you've obviously never researched the man behind the medicine." He eased Mari off him and sat up, his elbows on his knees as he hung his head, the weight of the memories too damn much. "The woman driving the other car was pregnant. She lost the baby."

"Oh, no, Rowan how tragic for her." Mari's voice filled with sadness and a hint of horror, but her hand fluttered to rest on his back. "And what a heavy burden for you to carry as the driver of the car."

She didn't know the half of it. No one did. To let the full extent of his guilt out would stain his brother's memory. Yet, for some reason he couldn't pinpoint, he found himself confessing all for the first time. To Mari. "But I wasn't driving."

Her hand slid up to rub the back of his neck and she sat up beside him, sheet clasped to her chest. "The news reports all say you were."

"That's what we told the police." He glanced over at her. "My brother and I both filled out formal statements saying I was the driver."

She stared back at him for two crashes of the waves before her eyes went wide with realization. "Your brother was actually the one behind the wheel that night? And he was drunk?"

Rowan nodded tightly. "We were both injured in the car accident, knocked out and rushed to the nearest hospital. When I woke up from surgery for a punctured lung, my mother was with me. My dad was with my brother, who'd broken his nose and fractured his jaw. They wanted us to get our stories straight before we talked to the police."

That night came roaring back to him, the confusion, the pain. The guilt that never went away no matter how many lives he saved at the clinic.

"Did your parents actually tell you to lie for your brother?" Her eyes went wider with horror. Clearly her parents would have never considered such a thing.

Most never would. He understood that, not that it made him feel one bit better about his own role in what had happened. She needed to understand the position they'd all been in, how he'd tried to salvage his brother's life only to make an even bigger mistake. One that cost him...too much.

"We were both drunk that night, but my brother was eighteen years old. I was only sixteen, a minor. The penalty would be less for me, but Dylan could serve hard time in jail. If I confessed to driving the car, Dylan could still have a future, a chance to turn his life around while he was still young."

"So you took the blame for your brother. You allowed yourself to be sentenced to a military reform school because your family pressured you, oh, Rowan…" She swept back his hair, her hands cool against his skin. "I am so sorry."

But he didn't want or deserve her comfort or sympathy. Rather than reject it outright, he linked fingers with her and lowered her arms.

"There was plenty of blame to go around that night. I could have made so many different choices. I could have called a cab at the party or asked someone else to drive us home." The flashing lights outside reminded him of the flash of headlights before the wreck, the blurred cop cars before he'd blacked out, then finally the arrival of the police to arrest him. "I wasn't behind the wheel, but I was guilty of letting my brother have those keys."

His brother had been a charismatic character, everyone believed him when he said he would change, and Rowan had gotten used to following his lead. When Dylan told him he was doing great in rehab, making his meetings, laying off the bottle, Rowan had believed him.

"What about your brother's guilt for what happened that night? Didn't Dylan deserve to pay for what happened to that woman, for you giving up your high school years?"

Trust Mari to see this analytically, to analyze it in clear-cut terms of rights and wrongs. Life didn't work that way. The world was too full of blurred gray territory.

"My brother paid plenty for that night and the decisions I made." If Rowan had made the right choices in the beginning, his brother would still be alive today. "Two years later, Dylan was in another drunk-driving accident. He drove his truck into the side of a house. He died." Rowan drew in a ragged breath, struggling like hell not to shrug off her touch that left him feeling too raw right now. "So you see, my decisions that night cost two lives."

Mari scooted to kneel in front of him, the sheet still clasped to her chest. Her dark hair spiraled around her shoulders in a wild sexy mess, but her amber eyes were no-nonsense. "You were sixteen years old and your parents pressured you to make the wrong decision. They sacrificed you to save your brother. They were wrong to do that."

Memories grated his insides, every word pouring acid on freshly opened wounds. He left the bed, left her, needing to put distance between himself and Mari's insistence.

He stepped over the tapestry pillows and yanked on his boxers. "You're not hearing me, Mari." He snagged his jeans from the floor and jerked them on one leg at a time. "I accept responsibility for my own actions. I wasn't a little kid. Blaming other people for our mistakes is a cop-out."

And the irony of it all, the more he tried to make amends, the more people painted him as some kind of freaking saint. He needed air. Now.

A ringing phone pierced the silence between them.

Not her ringtone. His, piping through the nursery monitor. Damn it. He'd left his cell phone in his room. "I should get that before it wakes the baby."

He hotfooted it out of her room, grateful for the excuse to escape more of her questions. Why the hell couldn't they just make love until the rest of the world faded away?

With each step out the door, he felt the weight of her gaze following him. He would have to give her some kind of closure to her questions, and he would. Once he had himself under control again.

He opened the door leading into his bedroom. His phone rang on the bamboo dresser near the bassinet. He grabbed the cell and took it back into the sitting area, reading the name scrolling across the screen.

Troy Donavan?

Premonition burned over him. His computer pal had to have found something big in order to warrant a call in the middle of the night.

Mari filled the doorway, tan satin sheet wrapped around her, toga-style. "Is something wrong?"

"I don't know yet." He thumbed the talk button on the cell phone. "Yes?"

"Hi, Rowan." Hillary's voice filled his ear. "It's me. Troy's found a trail connecting a worker at the hotel to a hospital record on one of the outlying islands— he's still working the data. But he's certain he's found Issa's mother."

Ten

Mari cradled sleeping Issa in her arms, rocking her for what would be the last time. She stared past the garland-draped minibar to the midday sun marking the passage of the day, sweeping away precious final minutes with this sweet child she'd already grown to love.

Her heart was breaking in two.

She couldn't believe her time with Issa was coming to an end. Before she'd even been able to fully process the fact that she'd actually followed through on the decision to sleep with Rowan, her world had been tossed into utter chaos with one phone call that swept Issa from them forever.

Troy Donavan had tracked various reflections of reflections in surveillance videos, piecing them together with some maze of other cameras in everything from banks to cops' radar to follow a path to a hint of a clue. They'd found the woman who'd walked away from the room-service trolley where Issa had been hidden. They'd gone a step further in the process to be sure. At some point, Mari had lost the thread of how he'd traced the trail back to a midwife on the mainland who'd delivered Issa. She'd been able to identify the mother, proving the baby's identity with footprint records.

The young mother had made her plan meticulously and worked to cover her tracks. She'd uncovered Rowan's schedule to speak at this conference then managed to get hired as a temp in the extra staff brought on for the holiday crowd. That's why she hadn't been on the employee manifest.

It appeared she'd had a mental breakdown shortly after leaving her child and was currently in a hospital. Issa had no grandparents, but she had a great aunt and uncle who wanted her. Deeply. In their fifties, their four sons were all grown but they hadn't hesitated in stepping up to care for their great niece. They owned a small coastal art gallery on the mainland and had plenty of parenting knowledge. They weren't wealthy, but their business and lives were stable.

All signs indicated they could give Issa a wonderful life full of love. Mari should be turning cartwheels over the news. So many orphans in Africa had no one to call their own and here Issa had a great family ready and eager to care for her.

Still, Mari could barely breathe at the prospect of handing over the baby, even though she knew this was the best thing for Issa.

The main door opened and Mari flinched, clutching the tiny girl closer. Rowan entered, lines fanning from his eyes attesting to the sleepless night they'd both endured after the fateful phone call about Issa's identity.

Rowan had scraped his hair back with a thin leather tie, his jeans and button-down shirt still sporting the wrinkles from when she'd tossed them aside in an effort to get him naked. That seemed eons ago now. Those moments after the call when they'd hastily gotten dressed again had passed in a frenzied haze.

"Any news?" she asked, feeling like a wretched person for hoping somehow she could keep Issa. She wasn't in any position to care for a baby. She'd never even given much thought to being a mother. But right now, it was the only thing she could think about. Who knew that a baby could fill a void in her life that she would have never guessed needed filling?

He shook his head and sat on the arm of the sofa near her, his blue eyes locked on the two of them. "Just more verification of what we learned last night. The mother's note was honest. Her husband was a soldier killed in a border dispute. And just more confirmation to what we already knew—she picked up a job doing temp work here, which is why she didn't show up on the initial employee search. The woman you saw that night running from the cart was, in fact, Issa's mother. She has family support back on the mainland. But it appears her husband's death hit her especially hard when she was already suffering from postpartum depression."

That last part hadn't been in the early reports. The whole issue became muddier now that the baby hadn't been left out of selfishness, but rather out of a deep mental illness. "Issa ended up in a room-service cart because of postpartum depression?"

"Approximately one in eight new mothers suffer from it in the States." He pinched the bridge of his nose as if battling a headache. "Even more so here with the rampant poverty and lack of medical care."

Mari's arms twitched protectively around the bundled infant. Would it have made a difference for Issa's mother if the family had been more supportive? Or had they been shut out? So many questions piled on top of each other until she realized she was simply looking for someone to blame, a reason why it would be okay to keep Issa. The scent of baby detergent—specially bought so she could wash the tiny clothes herself—mingled with sweet baby breath. Such a tender, dear bundle...

When Issa squirmed, Mari forced herself to relax—at least outwardly. "I guess I should be grateful she didn't harm her child. What happens now?"

Mari's eyes dropped to the child as Issa fought off sleep, her tiny fingers clenching and unclenching.

"She goes to her family," he said flatly.

"Where were they when Issa's mother felt so desperate?" The question fell from Mari's heart as much as her mouth, the objective scientist part of her nowhere to be found. She had to be certain before she could let go.

Rowan's hand fell to a tiny baby foot encased in a Christmas plaid sleeper. "The aunt and uncle insist they offered help, and that they didn't know how badly their niece was coping."

"Do you believe them?"

"They don't live nearby so it's entirely possible they missed the signs. Issa's only three months old." He patted the baby's chest once before shoving to his feet again, pacing restlessly. "They came for the funeral six weeks ago, left some money, followed up with calls, but she told them she was managing all right."

"And they believed her." How awful did it make her that she was still desperately searching for something to fault them for, some reason why they couldn't be the right people to raise the little angel in her arms.

"From everything our sources can tell, they're good people. Solid income from their tourist shop." He stopped at the window, palming the glass and leaning forward with a weary sigh. "They want custody of Issa and there's no legal or moral reason I can see why they shouldn't have her."

"What about what we want?" she asked quickly, in case she might have second thoughts and hold back the words.

"We don't have any rights to her." He glanced back over his shoulder. "This is the best scenario we could have hoped would play out. That first night when we spoke to the cops, we both never really dreamed this good of a solution could be found for her."

"I realize that… It's just…"

He turned to face her, leaning back and crossing his arms over his chest. "You already love her."

"Of course I care about her."

A sad half smile tipped his mouth. "That's not what I said."

"I've only known her a few days." Mari rolled out the logic as if somehow she could convince herself.

"I've watched enough new mothers in my line of work to know how fast the heart engages."

What did he hope to achieve by this? By stabbing her with his words? "I'm not her mother."

"You have been, though. You've done everything a mother would do to protect her child. It's not surprising you want to keep her."

Mari's throat clogged with emotion. "I'm in no position to take care of a baby. She has relatives who want her and can care for her. I know what I have to do."

"You're giving her the best chance, like a good mother." He cupped the back of her head, comfort in his gaze and in his touch.

She soaked up his supporting strength. "Are you trying to soften me up again?"

"I'm wounded you would think I'm that manipulative." He winked.

"Ha," she choked on a half laugh. "Now you're trying to make me smile so I won't cry."

He massaged her scalp lightly. "It's okay to cry if you need to."

She shook her head. "I think I'll just keep rocking her, maybe sing some Christmas carols until her family arrives. I know she won't remember me, but…"

A buzzer sounded at their suite door a second before Hillary walked in, followed by Troy. Mari sighed in relief over the brief reprieve. The aunt and uncle weren't here yet.

Hillary smiled gently. "The family is on their way up. I thought you would want the warning."

"Thank you for your help tracking them down." Mari could hardly believe she managed to keep her voice flat and unemotional in light of the caldron churning inside her.

Troy sat on the sofa beside his wife, the wiry computer mogul sliding an arm around Hillary's shoulders. "I'm glad we were able to resolve the issue so quickly."

Yet it felt like she'd spent a lifetime with Rowan and the baby.

Hillary settled into her husband's arm. "Mari, did Rowan tell you the tip that helped us put the pieces together came from the press coverage you brought in?"

"No, not that I remember." Although he might have

said something and she missed it. Since she'd heard Issa was leaving, Mari had been in a fog.

"Thanks to the huge interest your name inspired, we were contacted by a nurse whose story sounded legit. We showed her the composite sketch we'd pieced together from the different camera angles." Hillary rambled on, filling the tense silence. "She identified the woman as a patient she'd helped through delivery. From there, the rest of the pieces came together. She never would have heard about this if not for you and Rowan. You orchestrated this perfectly, Mari."

"With your help. Rowan is lucky to have such great friends."

And with those words she realized she didn't have people to reach out to in a crisis. She had work acquaintances, and she had family members she kept at arm's length. She spent her life focused on her lab. She'd sealed herself off from the world, running from meaningful relationships as surely as she ran from the press. Shutting herself away from her parents' disapproval—her father wanting her to assume her role of princess, her mother encouraging her to be a rebellious child embracing a universe beyond. Ultimately she'd disappointed them both. Rowan and this baby were her first deep connections in so long....

And it was tearing her apart to say goodbye to them.

She didn't want this pain. She wanted her safe world back. The quiet and order of her research lab, where she could quantify results and predict outcomes.

The buzzer sounded again and Mari bit her lip to keep from shouting in denial. Damn it, she would stay in control. She would see this through in a calm manner, do nothing to upset Issa.

Even though every cell in her cried out in denial.

* * *

Rowan watched helplessly as Mari passed the baby over to her relatives—a couple he'd made damn sure to investigate to the fullest. He'd relocated orphans countless times in his life and he'd always been careful, felt the weight of responsibility.

Never had that weight felt this heavy on his shoulders.

He studied the couple, in their fifties, the husband in a crisp linen suit, the wife in a colorful dress with a matching headscarf. The aunt took Issa from Mari's arms while the uncle held a diaper bag.

Mari twisted her hands in front of her, clearly resisting the temptation to yank the baby back. "She likes to be held close, but facing outward so she can see what's going on. And you have to burp her after every ounce of formula or she spits up. She likes music—"

Her voice cracked.

The aunt placed a hand on her arm. "Thank you for taking such good care of little Issa, Princess. If we had known about our niece's intentions, we would have volunteered to take Issa immediately. But when a young mother assures you she is fine, who would ever think to step in and offer to take her child? Trust us though, we will shower her with love. We will make sure she always knows you have been her guardian angel...."

With teary eyes, Mari nodded, but said nothing.

Troy stepped into the awkward silence. "My wife and I will escort you to your car through a back entrance to be sure the press doesn't overrun you."

Thank God, Troy quickly ushered them out before this hellish farewell tore them all in half. Rowan stole one last look at the baby's sweet chubby-cheeked face, swallowed hard and turned to Mari. No doubt she needed him more now.

The second the door closed behind the Donavans, Mari's legs folded.

She sank into the rocking chair again, nearly doubled over as she gulped in air. Her lovely face tensed with pain as she bit her lower lip. "Rowan, I don't think," she gasped, "I can't…I can't give my presentation this afternoon."

He understood the feeling. Rowan hooked his arm around her shoulders. "I'll call the conference coordinator. I'll tell them you're sick."

"But I'm never sick." She looked up at him with bemused eyes, bright with unshed tears. "I never bow out at work. What's wrong with me?"

"You're grieving." So was he. Something about this child was different, maybe because of the role she'd played in bringing Mari to him. Maybe because of the Christmas season. Or perhaps simply because the little tyke had slipped past the defenses he worked so hard to keep in place as he faced year after year of treating bone-crushing poverty and sickness. "You're human."

"I only knew her a few days. She's not my child…." Mari pressed a hand to her chest, rubbing a wound no less deep for not being visible. "I shouldn't be this upset."

"You loved her—you still do." He shifted around to kneel in front of her, stroking her face, giving Mari comfort—a welcome distraction when he needed it most. "That's clear to anyone who saw you with her."

"I know, damn it." She blinked back tears. "I don't want to think about it. I don't want to feel any of this. I just need…this."

Mari grabbed his shirt front, twisted her fist in the

fabric and yanked him toward her as she fell into him. Rowan absorbed their fall with his body, his shoulders meeting the thick carpet. Mari blanketed him, her mouth meeting his with a frenzy and intensity there was no denying. She'd found an outlet for her grief and he was damn well ready to help her with that. They both needed this.

Needed an outlet for all the frustrated emotions roaring through the room.

She wriggled her hips erotically against his ready arousal. A moan of pleasure slipped from her lips as she nipped his ear. There was no need to be silent any longer. Their suite was empty. Too empty. Their first encounter had been focused on staying quiet, in control as they discovered each other for the first time.

Tonight, control didn't exist.

He pushed those thoughts away and focused on Mari, on making sure she was every bit as turned on as he was. He gathered the hem of her dress and bunched it until he found the sweet curve of her bottom. He guided her against him, met her with a rolling rhythm of his own, a synchronicity they'd discovered together last night.

Sitting up, increasing the pressure against his erection, she yanked his shirt open, buttons popping free and flying onto the carpet. Her ragged breathing mingled with his. He swept her dress off and away until she wore only a pale green satin bra and underwear. He was quickly realizing her preference for soft, feminine lingerie and he enjoyed peeling it from her. He flung the bra to rest on the bar. Then twisted his fist in her panties until the thin strap along her hip snapped. The last scrap of fabric fell away.

She clasped his head in her hands and drew his face

to her breasts. Her guidance, her demands, made him even harder. He took her in his mouth, enjoying the giving as much as the taking. Her moans and sighs were driving him wild. And yes, he had his own pent-up frustrations to work out, his own regret over seeing Issa leave… He shut down those thoughts, grounding himself in the now.

Arching onto her heels, Mari fumbled with the fly of his pants.

"Condom," he groaned. "In my pocket."

He lifted his butt off the floor and she stroked behind him to pluck the packet free. Thank heaven he'd thought to keep one on him even in a crisis. Because he couldn't stomach the thought of stopping, not even for an instant.

Then he felt her hands on him, soft, stroking. He throbbed at her touch as she sheathed him in the condom, then took him inside her. His head dug back as he linked fingers with her, following the ride where she took him, hard and fast, noisy and needy. The fallout would have to take care of itself, because right now, they were both locked in a desperate drive to block out the pain of loss.

Already, he could feel the building power of his release rolling through him. He gritted his teeth, grinding back the need to come. Reaching between them to ease her over the edge with him. One look at her face, the crescendo of her sweet cries, told him she was meeting him there now. He thrust, again and again until his orgasm throbbed free while hers pulsed around him.

He caught her as she collapsed into his arms. He soaked in the warmth of her skin, the pounding of her heart—hell, everything about her.

The cooling air brought hints of reality slithering

back, the world expanding around them. The roaring in his ears grew louder, threatening this pocket of peace. It was too soon for him to take her again, but that didn't rule out other pleasurable possibilities.

Rowan eased Mari from him and onto her back. He kissed her mouth, her jaw, along her neck, inhaling the floral essence of her. Her hands skimmed up and down his spine as she reclined languidly. Smiling against her skin, he nipped his way lower, nuzzling and stroking one breast then the other.

"Rowan?"

"Shhh…" He blew across her damp nipple. The damp brown tip pebbled even tighter for him and he took her in his mouth, flicking with his tongue.

He sprinkled kisses along the soft underside, then traveled lower, lower still until he parted her legs and stroked between her thighs, drawing a deep sigh from her. He dipped his head and breathed in the essence of her, tasted her. Teased at the tight bundle of nerves until she rambled a litany of need for more. He was more than happy to comply.

A primitive rush of possession surged through him. She was his. He cupped the soft globes of her bottom and brought her closer to him, circled and laved, worked her until her fingers knotted restlessly in his hair. He took her to the edge of completion again, then held back, taking her to the precipice again and again, knowing her orgasm would be all the more powerful with the build.

Her head thrashed against the carpet and she cried out his name as her release gripped her. Her hands flung out, knocking over an end table, sending a lamp crashing to the floor.

He watched the flush of completion spread over her

as he slid back up to lay beside her. The evening breeze drifted over them, threatening to bring reality with it.

There was only one way to make it through the rest of this night. Make love to Mari until they both collapsed with exhaustion. Rolling to his knees, he slid his arms under her, lifting as he stood. He secured her against his chest, the soft give of her body against his stirring him.

Her arm draped around his neck, her head lolling against him as she still breathed heavily in the aftermath of her release. He strode across the suite toward his bedroom, his jeans open and riding low on his hips. Hell, he'd never even gotten his pants off.

He lowered Mari to his bed, the sight of her naked body, long legs and subtle curves stirring him impossibly hard again. Shadows played along her dusky skin, inviting him to explore. To lose himself in the oblivion of her body. To forget for a few hours that the emptiness of their suite was so damn tangible… No baby sighs. No iPhone of Christmas lullabies. Gone.

Just like Issa. Their reason for staying together.

Eleven

Mari had spent a restless night in Rowan's arms. As the morning light pierced through the shutters, he'd suggested they get away from the resort and all the memories of Issa that lurked in their suite. She hadn't even hesitated at jumping on board with his plan.

Literally.

Mari stretched out on the bow of the sailboat and stared up at the cloudless sky, frigate birds gliding overhead with their wide wings extended full-out. Waves slapped against the hull, and lines pinged against the mast. Rowan had leased the thirty-three-foot luxury sailboat for the two of them to escape for the day to a deserted shore. No worries about the press spying on them and no reminders of the baby. Nothing to do but to stare into the azure waters, watching fish and loggerhead turtles.

God, how she needed to get away from the remind-

ers. Her time with the baby had touched her heart and
made her realize so many things were missing in her
life. Love. Family. She'd buried herself in work, retreating into a world that made sense to her after a lifetime
of feeling awkward in her own skin. But holding that
sweet little girl had made Mari accept she'd turned her
back on far too much.

That didn't mean she had any idea how to fix it. Or
herself. She watched Rowan guiding the sailboat, open
shirt flapping behind him, sun burnishing his blond
hair.

Rowan had made love to her—and she to him—
until they'd both fallen into an exhausted sleep. They'd
slept, woken only long enough to order room service
and made love again. She had the feeling Rowan was
as confused and empty as she, but she couldn't quite
put her finger on why.

For that matter, maybe she was just too lost in her
own hurt to understand his.

In the morning, he'd told her to dress for a day on a
boat. She hadn't questioned him, grateful for the distraction. Mari had tossed on a sarong, adding dark
glasses and an old-school Greta Garbo scarf to make
her escape. He'd surprised her with a gift, bracelets
she'd admired at the marketplace their first night out
with Issa. She stretched her arm out, watching the sun
refract off the silver bangles and colorful beads.

Rowan sailed the boat, handling the lines with ease
as the hull chopped through the water toward an empty
cove, lush mountains jutting in the distance. They'd followed the coast all morning toward a neighboring island with a private harbor. If only the ache in her heart
was as easy to leave behind.

She rolled to her tummy and stretched out along her

towel, her well-loved body languid and a bit stiff. Chin on her hands, she gazed out at the rocks jutting from the water along the secluded coastline. She watched the gannets and petrels swoop and dive for fish. Palm trees clustered along the empty shoreline, creating a thick wall of foliage just beyond the white sandy beaches. Peaceful perfection, all familiar and full of childhood memories of vacationing along similar shores with her parents.

A shadow stretched across her, a broad-shouldered shadow. She flipped to her back again, shading her eyes to look up at Rowan. "Shouldn't you be at the helm?"

"We've dropped anchor." He crouched beside her, too handsome for his own good in swim trunks and an open shirt, ocean breeze pulling at his loose hair. "Come with me and have something to drink?"

She clasped his outstretched hand and stood, walking with him, careful to duck and weave past the boom and riggings. The warm hardwood deck heated her bare feet. "You didn't have to be so secretive about our destination."

"I wanted to surprise you." He jumped down to the deck level, grasping her waist and lowering her to join him. He gestured to where he'd poured them two glasses of mango juice secured in the molded surface between the seat cushions, the pitcher tucked securely in an open cooler at his bare feet.

"That's your only reason?"

"I wasn't sure you would agree, and we both needed to get away from the resort." He passed her a glass, nudging her toward the captain's chair behind the wheel. "Besides, my gorgeous, uptight scientist, you need to have fun."

"I have fun." Sitting, she sipped her drink. The sweet

natural sugars sent a jolt of energy through her, his words putting her on the defensive. "My work is fun."

He cocked an eyebrow, shooting just above his sunglasses.

"Okay, my work is rewarding. And I don't recall being all that uptight when I was sitting on the bar last night." She eyed him over the glass.

"Fair enough. I'm taking you out because I want you mellow and softened up so when I try to seduce you later you completely succumb to my charm." He thudded the heel of his palm to his forehead, clearly doing his best to take her mind off things. "Oh, wait, I already seduced you."

"Maybe I seduced you." She tossed aside her sunglasses and pulled off his aviator shades, her bracelets chiming with each movement. She leaned in to kiss him, more than willing to be distracted from the questions piling up in her mind.

Like where they would go from here once the conference was over. Since she didn't have any suggestions in mind, she sure wasn't going to ask for his opinion.

"Whose turn is it, then, to take the initiative?" He pulled her drink from her and stepped closer.

"I've lost count." She let her eyes sweep over him seductively, immersing herself in this game they both played, delaying the inevitable.

"Princess, you do pay the nicest compliments." He stroked her face, along the scarf holding back her hair, tugging it free.

"You say the strangest things." She traced his mouth, the lips that had brought her such pleasure last night.

"We're here to play, not psychoanalyze."

Her own lips twitched with a self-deprecating smile. "Glad to know it, because I stink at reading people."

"Why do you assume that?" His question mingled with the call of birds in the trees and the plop of fish.

"Call it a geek thing."

"You make geek sexy." He nipped her tracing finger, then sucked lightly.

She rolled her eyes. "You are such a…"

"A what?"

"I don't even have words for you."

His eyes went serious for the first time this morning. "Glad to know I mystify you as much as you bemuse me."

"I've always thought of myself as a straightforward person. Some call that boring." She flinched, hating the feeling that word brought, knowing she couldn't—wouldn't—change. "For me, there's comfort in routine."

Those magnificently blue eyes narrowed and darkened. "Tell me who called you boring and I'll—"

She clapped a hand over his mouth, bracelets dangling. "It's okay. But thanks." She pulled her hand away, a rogue wave bobbing the boat beneath her. "I had trouble making friends in school. I didn't fit in for so many reasons—everything from my ridiculous IQ to the whole princess thing. I was either much younger than my classmates or they were sucking up because of my family. There was no sisterhood for me. It was tough for people to see the real me behind all that clutter."

"I wasn't an instant fit at school, either." He shifted to stand beside her, looping an arm around her shoulders bared by the sarong.

She leaned against him, looking out over the azure blue waters. The continent of her birth was such a mixture of lush magnificence and stark poverty. "You don't need to change your history to make me feel better. I'm okay with myself."

"God's honest truth here." He rested his chin on top of her head. "My academy brothers and I were all misfits. The headmaster there did a good job at redirecting us, channeling us, helping us figure out ways to put our lives on the right path again."

"All of you? That's quite a track record."

He went still against her. "Not all of us. Some of us were too far gone to be rehabilitated." His sigh whispered over her, warmer than the sun. "You may have read in the news about Malcolm Douglas's business manager—he was a schoolmate of ours. He lost his way, forgot about rules and integrity. He did some shady stuff to try and wrangle publicity for his client."

"Your friend. Malcolm. Another of your Brotherhood?"

"Malcolm and I aren't as close as I am to the others. But yes, he's a friend." He turned her by her shoulders and stared into her eyes. "We're not perfect, any of us, but the core group of us, we can call on each other for anything, anytime."

"Like how the casino owner friend provided the start-up money for your clinic…"

Rowan had built an incredible support system for himself after his parents failed him. While she'd cut herself off from the world.

"That he did. You wouldn't recognize Conrad from the high school photos. He was gangly and wore glasses back then, but he was a brilliant guy and he knew it. Folks called him Mr. Wall Street, because of his dad and how Conrad used his trust fund to manipulate the stock market to punish sweatshop businesses."

"You all may have been misfits, but it appears you share a need for justice."

"We didn't all get along at first. I was different

from them, though, or so I liked to tell myself. I didn't come from money like most of the guys there—or like you—and I wasn't inordinately talented like Douglas. I thought I was better than those overprivileged brats."

"Yet, Conrad must respect you to have invested so much money to start the clinic."

"If we're going to be honest—" he laughed softly "—I'm where I am today because of a cookie."

"A cookie?" She tipped her head back to the warm sunshine, soaking in the heat of the day and the strength of the man beside her.

"My mom used to send me these care packages full of peanut-butter cookies with M&M's baked into them." His eyes took on a faraway look and a fond smile.

Mari could only think that same mother had sent him to that school in his brother's place. Those cookies must have tasted like dust in light of such a betrayal from the woman who should have protected him. She bit back the urge to call his mother an unflattering name and just listened, ocean wind rustling her hair.

"One day, I was in my bunk, knocking back a couple of those cookies while doing my macro biology homework." He toyed with the end of her scarf. "I looked up to find Conrad staring at those cookies like they were caviar. I knew better than to offer him one. His pride would have made him toss it back in my face."

She linked fingers with him and squeezed as he continued, her cheek against the warm cotton of his shirt, her ear taking in the steady thrum of his heart.

"We were all pretty angry at life in those days. But I had my cookies and letters from Mom to get me through the days when I didn't think I could live with the guilt of what I'd done."

What his family had done. His mother, father and his brother. Why couldn't he see how they'd sacrificed him?

"But back to Conrad. About a week later, I was on my way to the cafeteria and I saw him in the visitation area with his dad. I was jealous as hell since my folks couldn't afford to fly out to visit me—and then I realized he and his dad were fighting."

"About what?" She couldn't help but ask, desperate for this unfiltered look into the teenage Rowan, hungry for insights about what had shaped him into the man he'd become.

"From what Conrad shouted, it was clear his father wanted him to run a scam on Troy's parents and convince them to invest in some bogus company or another. Conrad decked his dad. It took two security guards to pull him off."

Hearing the things that Rowan and his friends had been through as teens, she felt petty for her anger over her own childhood. The grief Rowan and his friends had faced, the storms in their worlds, felt so massive in comparison to her own. She had two parents that loved her, two homes, and yes, she was shuttled back and forth, but in complete luxury.

"And the cookie?"

"I'm getting there." He sketched his fingers up and down her bare arm. "Conrad spent a couple of days in the infirmary—his dad hit him back and dislocated Conrad's shoulder. The cops didn't press charges on the old man because the son threw the first punch. Anyhow, Conrad's first day out of the infirmary, I felt bad for him so I wrapped a cookie in a napkin and put it on his bunk. He didn't say anything, but he didn't toss it back in my face, either." He threw his hands wide. "And here I am today."

Her heart hurt so badly she could barely push words out. "Why are you telling me this?"

"I don't know. I just want you to understand why my work is so important to me, so much so that I couldn't have kept Issa even if her family didn't come through. Because if I start keeping every orphan that tugs at my emotions, I won't be able to sustain all I've fought so hard to build. The clinic…it's everything to me. It helps me fill the hole left by Dylan's death, helps me make up for the lives lost."

She heard him, heard an isolation in his words in spite of all those friends. He'd committed himself to a life of service that left him on a constant, lonely quest. And right then and there, her soul ached for him.

She slid her hand up into his hair, guiding his mouth to hers. He stepped between her knees, and she locked her arms around his neck. Tight. Demanding and taking.

"Now," she whispered against his mouth, fishing in his back pocket for a condom.

He palmed her knees apart and she purred her approval. Her fingers made fast work of his swim trunks, freeing his erection and sheathing him swiftly, surely.

She locked her legs around his waist and drew him in deeper. He drove into her again and again. She angled back, gripping the bar, bracelets sliding down to collect along her hand. He took in the beauty of her, her smooth skin, pert breasts, her head thrown back and hair swaying with every thrust. The boat rocked in a rhythm that matched theirs as his shouts of completion twined and mingled with hers, carried on the breeze.

In that moment she felt connected to him more than physically. She identified with him, overwhelmed by an understanding of him being as alone in the world as her. But also hammered by a powerlessness to change that. His vision and walls were as strong as hers, always had been. Maybe more so.

What a time to figure out she might have sacrificed too much for her work—only realizing that now, as she fell for a man who would sacrifice anything for *his*.

The taste of the sea, sweat and Mari still clinging to his skin, Rowan opened the door to their suite the next morning, praying the return to land and real life wouldn't bring on the crushing sense of loss. He'd hoped to distract her from Issa—and also find some way to carve out a future for them. They were both dedicated to their work. They could share that, even in their disagreements. They could use that as a springboard to work out solutions. Together. His time with her overnight on the sailboat had only affirmed that for him.

He just hoped he'd made a good start in persuading Mari of the same thing.

Guiding her into the suite with a hand low on her spine, he stepped deeper into the room. Only to stop short. His senses went on alert. There was someone here.

Damn it, there was more traffic through this supposedly secure room than through the lobby. Which of course meant it was one of his friends.

Elliot Starc rose from the sofa and from Mari's gasp beside him, clearly she recognized the world-famous race-car driver...and underwear model.

Rowan swallowed a curse. "Good morning, Elliot. Did you get booted out of your own room?"

Laughing, Elliot took Mari's hand lightly and ignored Rowan's question. "Princess, it's an honor to meet you."

"Mr. Starc, you're one of Rowan's Brotherhood friends, I assume."

Elliot's eyebrows shot up. "You told her?"

"We talk." Among other things.

"Well, color me stunned. That baby was lucky to have landed in Rowan's room. Our Interpol connections kept all of you safe while bringing this to a speedy conclusion."

Crap. The mention of Interpol hung in the air, Mari's eyes darting to his.

Oblivious to the gaffe, Elliot continued, "Which brings me to my reason for being here. I've emailed a summary of the existing security detail, but I need to get back to training, get my mind back in the game so I don't set more than my hair on fire."

Rowan pulled a tight smile. "Thanks, buddy."

Mari frowned. "Interpol?"

Elliot turned sharply to Rowan. "You said you told her about the Brotherhood."

"Classmates. I told her we're classmates." He didn't doubt she would keep his secret safe, but knowing wouldn't help her and anything that didn't help was harmful. "You, my friend, made a mighty big assumption for someone who should know better."

"She's a princess. You've been guarding her." Elliot scratched his sheared hair. "I thought... Ah, hell. Just..." Throwing his hands out and swiping the air as if that explained it all, Elliot spun on his heel and walked out the door.

Mari sat hard, sinking like a stone on the edge of the sofa. "You're with Interpol?" She huffed on a long sigh. "Of course you're with Interpol."

"I'm a physician. That's my primary goal, my mission in life." He paused, unable to dodge the truth as he kneeled in front of her. "But yes, I help out Interpol on occasion with freelance work in the area. No one thinks twice about someone like me wandering around wealthy fundraisers or traveling to remote countries."

He could see her closing down, pulling away.

"Mari?"

"It's your job. I understand."

"Are you angry with me for not telling you?"

"Why would you? It's not my secret to know. Your friend…he assumed more about us than he should. But you know I won't say a word. I understand well what it's like to be married to your work."

Her words came out measured and even, her body still, her spine taking on that regal "back off" air that shouted of generations of royalty. "Mari, this doesn't have to mean things change between us. If anything we can work together."

"Work, right…" Her amber eyes flickered with something he couldn't quite pin down.

"Are you all right?"

"I'll be fine. It's all just a lot to process, this today. Issa yesterday."

He cradled her shoulders in his hands. She eased away.

"Mari, it's okay to shout at me if you're mad. Or to cry about Issa. I'm here for you," he said, searching for the right way to approach her.

"Fine. You want me to talk? To yell? You've got it. I would appreciate your acting like we're equal rather than stepping into your benevolent physician shoes because no one would dare to contradict the man who does so much for the world." She shrugged free of his grip.

"Excuse me for trying to be a nice guy." He held up his hands.

"You're always the nice guy." She shot to her feet. "The saint. Giving out comfort, saving the world, using that as a wall between you and other people."

"What the hell are you talking about?" He stood warily, watching her pace.

"There you go. Get mad at me." She stopped in front of him, crossing her arms over her chest. "At least real emotions put us on an even footing. Oh, wait, we're not even. You're the suave doctor/secret agent. I'm the awkward genius who locks herself away in a lab."

"Are we really returning to the old antagonistic back-and-forth way of communicating?" he asked. Her words felt damn unfair when he was working his tail off to help her through a rough time. "I thought we'd moved past that."

"That's not what I'm talking about and you know it. You're a smart man."

"Actually, you're the certified genius here. How about you explain it to me."

"You want me to cry and grieve and open myself up to you." She jabbed his chest with one finger, her voice rising with every word. "But what about you? When do you open up to me? When are you going to give me something besides the saintly work side of your life?"

"I've told you things about my past," he answered defensively.

"To be fair, yes you have," she conceded without backing down. "Some things. Certainly not everything. And when have you let me in? You're fine with things as long as you're the one doling out comfort. But accepting it? No way. Like now. You have every reason to grieve for Issa."

"She's in good hands, well cared for," he said through gritted teeth.

"See? There you go doing just what I said. You want me to cry and be emotional, but you—" she waved a hand "—you're just fine. Did you even allow yourself to grieve for your brother?"

His head snapped back, her words smacking him even as she kept her hands fisted at her sides. "Don't you dare use my brother against me. That has nothing to do with what we're discussing now."

"It has everything to do with what we're talking about. But if I'm mistaken, then explain it to me. Explain what you're feeling."

She waited while he searched for the right words, but everything he'd offered her so far hadn't worked. He didn't have a clue what to say to reassure her. And apparently he waited too long.

"That's what I thought." She shook her head sadly, backing away from him step by step. "I'm returning to my old room. There's no reason for me to be here anymore."

She spun away, the hem of her sarong fluttering as she raced into her room and slammed the door. He could hear her tossing her suitcase on the bed. Heard her muffled sobs. And heard the click of the lock that spoke loud and clear.

He'd blown it. Royally, so to speak. He might be confused about a lot of things. But one was crystal clear.

He was no longer welcome in Mari's life.

Twelve

The conference was over. Her week with Rowan was done.

Mari stood in front of the mirrored vanity and tucked the final pin into her hair, which was swept back in a sleek bun. Tonight's ball signified an official end to their time together. There was no dodging the event without being conspicuous and stirring up more talk in the press.

As if there wasn't enough talk already. At least all reports from the media—and from Rowan's Interpol friends—indicated that Issa was adapting well in her new home after only a couple of days. Something to be eternally grateful for. A blessing in this heartbreaking week.

Her pride demanded she finish with her head held high.

After her confrontation with Rowan, she'd waited the

remainder of her stay, hoping he would fight for her as hard as he fought for his work, for every person who walked through those clinic doors. But she hadn't heard a word from him since she'd stormed from his room and she'd gone back to her simple room a floor below. How easily he'd let her go, and in doing so, broken her heart.

But his ability to disconnect with her also filled her with resolve.

She wouldn't be like him anymore, hiding from the world. She was through staying in the shadows for fear of disappointing people.

Mari smoothed her hands down the shimmering red strapless dress, black swirls through the fabric giving the impression of phantom roses. The dress hugged her upper body, fitted past her hips then swept to the ground with a short train. It was a magnificent gown. She'd never worn anything like it. She would have called it a Cinderella moment except she didn't want to be some delicate princess at the ball. She was a one-day queen, boldly stepping into her own.

Her hands fell to the small tiara, diamonds refracting the vanity lights. Carefully, she tucked the crown—symbolic of so much more—on her head.

Stepping from her room, she checked the halls and, how ironic, for once the corridor was empty. No fans to carefully maneuver. She could make her way to the brass-plated elevator in peace.

Jabbing the elevator button, she curled her toes in her silken ballet slippers. Her stomach churned with nerves over facing the crowd downstairs alone, even more than that, over facing Rowan again. But she powered on, one leather-clad foot at a time. While she was ready to meet the world head-on in her red Vera Wang, she wasn't prepared to do so wearing high heels that would likely send her stumbling down the stairs.

She was bold, but practical.

Finally, the elevator doors slid open, except the elevator wasn't empty. Her stomach dropped in shock faster than a cart on a roller-coaster ride.

"Papa?" She stared at her father, her royal father.

But even more surprising, her mother stood beside him. "Going down, dear?"

Stunned numb, she stepped into the elevator car, brass doors sliding closed behind her.

"Mother, why are you and Papa here? *Together?*" she squeaked as her mom hugged her fast and tight.

The familiar scent of her mom's perfume enveloped her, like a bower of gardenias. And her mom wasn't dressed for a simple visit. Susan Mandara was decked out for the ball in a Christmas-green gown, her blond hair piled on top of her head. Familiar, yet so unusual, since Mari couldn't remember the last time she'd seen Adeen and Susan Mandara standing side by side in anything other than old pictures.

Her father kissed her on the forehead. "Happy Christmas, little princess."

She clutched her daddy's forearms, the same arms that used to toss her high in the air as a child. Always catching her.

Tonight, her father wore a tuxedo with a crimson tribal robe over it, trimmed in gold. As a child, she used to sneak his robes out to wear for dress-up with her parents laughing, her mother affectionately calling him Deen, her nickname for him. She'd forgotten that happy memory until just now.

Her mother smoothed cool hands over her daughter's face. "Your father and I have a child together." She gave

Mari's face a final pat. "Deen and I are bonded for life, *by* life, through you. We came to offer support and help you with all the press scrutiny."

Did they expect her to fail? She couldn't resist saying, "Some of this togetherness would have been welcome when I was younger."

"We've mellowed with age." Susan stroked her daughter's forehead. "I wish we could have given you a simpler path. We certainly wanted to."

If her mother had wanted to keep things simple, marrying a prince was surely a weird way to go about it.

Her father nodded his head. "You look magnificent. You are everything I wanted my princess to grow up to be."

"You're just saying that because I'm decked out in something other than a sack," she teased him, even though her heart ached with the cost of her newfound confidence. "But I can assure you, I still detest ribbon cuttings and state dinners."

"And you still care about the people. You'll make your mark in a different manner than I did. That's good." He held out both elbows as the elevator doors slid open on the ground floor. "Ladies? Shall we?"

Decorations in the hallway had doubled since she went upstairs to change after the final presentation of the day. Mari strode past oil palm trees decorated with bells. Music drifted from the ballroom, a live band played carols on flutes, harps and drums.

The sounds of Christmas. The sounds of home. Tables laden with food. She could almost taste the sweet cookies and the meats marinated in *chakalaka*.

A few steps later, she stood on the marble threshold of the grand ballroom. All eyes turned to her and for a moment her feet stayed rooted to the floor. Cameras clicked and she didn't so much as flinch or cringe. She wasn't sure what to do next as she swept the room with her eyes, taking in the ballroom full of medical professionals decked out in all their finery, with local bigwigs in attendance, as well.

Then her gaze hitched on Rowan, wearing a traditional tuxedo, so handsome he took her breath away.

His hair was swept back, just brushing his collar, his eyes blue flames that singed her even from across the room. She expected him to continue ignoring her. But he surprised her by striding straight toward her. All eyes followed him, and her heart leaped into her throat.

Rowan stopped in front of them and nodded to her father. "Sir, I believe your daughter and I owe the media a dance."

Owe the media?

What about what they owed each other?

And how could he just stand there as if nothing had happened between them, as if they hadn't bared their bodies and souls to each other? She had a gloriously undignified moment of wanting to kick him. But this was her time to shine and she refused to let him wreck it. She stepped into his arms, and he gestured to the band. They segued into a rendition of "Ave Maria," with a soloist singing.

Her heart took hope that he'd chosen the piece for her. He led her to the middle of the dance floor. Other couples melted away and into the crowd, leaving them alone, at the mercy of curious eyes and cameras.

As she allowed herself to be swept into his arms— into the music—she searched for something to say. "I appreciate the lovely song choice."

"It fits," he answered, but his face was still creased in a scowl, his eyes roving over her.

"Don't you like the dress?"

"I like the woman in the dress," he said hoarsely. "If you'd been paying attention, you would have realized my eyes have been saying that for a long time before you changed up your wardrobe."

"So why are you scowling?"

"Because I want this whole farce of a week to be over."

"Oh," she said simply, too aware of his hand on her waist, his other clasping her fingers.

"Do you believe me? About the dress, I mean." His feet moved in synch with hers, their bodies as fluid on the dance floor as they'd been making love.

"We've exchanged jabs in the past, insults even, but you've always been honest."

"Then why are you still sleeping on another floor of the hotel?"

"Oh, Rowan," she said bittersweetly. "Sex isn't the problem between us."

"Remind me what is?"

"The way you close people—me—out. It took me a long time to realize I'm deserving of everything. And so are you."

"I guess there's nothing left to say then."

The music faded away, and with a final sweep across the floor he stopped in front of her parents.

Rowan passed her hand back to her father. "With all due respect, sir, take better care of her."

Her mother smothered a laugh.

Her father arched a royal eyebrow. "I beg your pardon."

"More security detail. She's a princess. She deserves to be cared for and protected like one."

With a final nod, Rowan turned away and melted into the crowd and out of her life.

Five hours later, Mari hugged her pillow to her chest, watching her mom settle into the other double bed in the darkened room. "Mother, aren't we wealthy enough for you to have a suite or at least a room of your own?"

Susan rolled to her side, facing her daughter in the shadowy room lit only by moonlight streaming in. "I honestly thought you would be staying with Dr. Boothe even though this room was still booked in your name. And even with the show of good faith your father and I have given, we're not back to sharing a room."

Curtains rustled with the night ocean breeze and sounds of a steel-drum band playing on the beach for some late-night partiers.

"Rowan and I aren't a couple anymore." Although the haunting beauty of that dance still whispered through her, making her wonder what more she could have done. "It was just a…fling."

The most incredible few days of her life.

"Mari dear, you are not the fling sort," her mother reminded her affectionately. "So why are you walking away from him?"

Tears clogged her throat. "I'm honestly too upset to talk about this." She flipped onto her back, clenching her fists against the memory of his tuxedoed shoulders under her hands.

The covers rustled across the room as her mother sat up. "I made the biggest mistake of my life when I was about your age."

"Marrying my father. Yeah, I got that." Was it in her DNA to fail at relationships? Her parents had both been divorced twice.

"No, marrying the man I loved—your father— was the right move. Thinking I could change him? I screwed up there." She hugged her knees to her chest, her graying blond hair trailing down her back. "Before you think I'm taking all the blame here, he thought I would change, as well. So the divorce truly was a fifty- fifty screw-up on our part. He should have realized my free spirit is what he fell in love with and I should have recognized how drawn I was to his devotion to his country."

What was her mother trying to tell her? She wanted to understand, to step outside of the awkwardness in more ways than just being comfortable in a killer red dress. Except her mom was talking about not chang- ing at all.

"You're going to have to spell it out for me more clearly."

"Your father and I weren't a good couple. We weren't even particularly good at being parents. But, God, you sure turned out amazing," her mother said with an un- mistakable pride, soothing years of feeling like a dis- appointment. "Deen and I did some things right, and maybe if we'd focused more on the things we did right, we might have lasted."

Mari ached to pour out all the details of her fight with Rowan, how she needed him to open up. And how ironic was it that he accused her of not venting her emo- tions? Her thoughts jumbled together until she blurted out in frustration, "Do you know how difficult it is to love a saint?"

Her mother reached out in the dark, across the divide between their beds. "You love him?"

Mari reached back and clasped her mother's hand.

"Of course I do. I just don't know how to get through to him."

"You two have been a couple for—what?—a week? Seems to me like you're giving up awful fast."

Mari bristled defensively. "I've known him for years. And it's been an intense week."

"And you're giving that up? I'd so hoped you would be smarter than I was." Her mom gave her hand a final squeeze. "Think about it. Good night, Mari."

Long into the night, Mari stared out the window at the shoreline twinkling with lighted palm trees. The rolling waves crashed a steady reminder of her day sailing with Rowan. He'd done so much to comfort her. Not just with words, but with actions, by planning the day away from the hotel and painful memories.

What had she done for him?

Nothing.

She'd simply demanded her expectations for him rather than accepting him as he was. He'd accepted and appreciated her long before a ball gown. Even when he disagreed with her, he'd respected her opinion.

Damn it all, she *was* smarter than this. Of course Rowan had built walls around himself. Every person in his family had let him down—his parents and his brother. None of them had ever put him or his well-being first. Sure, he'd made friends with his school-mates, but he'd even admitted to feeling different from them.

Now she'd let him down, as well. He'd reached out to her as best he could and she'd told him what he of-fered wasn't good enough, maybe because she'd been scared of not being enough for him.

But she knew better than that now. A confidence flowed through her like a calming breeze blowing in off the ocean. With that calm came the surety of what to do next.

It was time to fight for the man she loved, a man she loved for his every saintly imperfection.

Rowan had always been glad to return to his clinic on the mainland. He'd spent every Christmas here in surgical scrubs taking care of patients since moving to Africa. He welcomed the work, leaving holiday celebrations to people with families.

Yet, for some reason, the CD of Christmas carols and a pre-lit tree in the corner didn't stir much in the way of festive feelings this year. A few gifts remained for the patients still in the hospital, the other presents having been passed out earlier, each box a reminder of shopping with Mari.

So he buried himself in work.

Phone tucked under his chin, he listened to Elliot's positive update on Issa, followed by a rambling recounting of his Australian Christmas vacation. Rowan cranked back in a chair behind his desk, scanning a computer file record on a new mother and infant due to be discharged first thing in the morning.

One wing of the facility held a thirty-bed hospital unit and the other wing housed a clinic. Not overly large, but all top-of-the-line and designed for efficiency. They doled out anything from vaccinations to prenatal care to HIV/AIDS treatment.

The most gut-wrenching of all? The patients who came for both prenatal care and HIV treatment. There was a desperate need here and he couldn't help everyone, but one at a time, he was doing his damnedest.

The antibacterial scent saturated each breath he took. Two nurses chatted with another doctor at the station across the hall. Other than that, the place was quiet as a church mouse this late at night.

"Elliot, if you've got a point here, make it. I've got a Christmas Eve dinner to eat."

Really, just a plate to warm in the microwave but he wasn't particularly hungry anyhow. Visions of Mari in that red gown, cloaked in total confidence, still haunted his every waking and sleeping thought. He'd meant what he'd said when he told her it didn't matter to him what clothes she wore. But he was damn proud of the peace she seemed to have found with being in the spotlight. Too bad he couldn't really be a part of it.

"Ah, Rowan, I really thought you were smarter than me, brother," Elliot teased over the phone from his Australian holiday. The background echoed with drunken carolers belting out a raucous version of "The Twelve Days of Christmas."

"As I recall, our grades were fairly on par with each other back in the day."

"Sure, but I've had about four concussions since then, not to mention getting set on fire."

A reluctant smile tugged at Rowan. "Your point?"

"Why in the hell did you let that woman go?" Elliot asked, the sounds of laughter and splashing behind him. "You're clearly crazy about her and she's nuts about you. And the chemistry… Every time you looked at each other, it was all I could do not to shout at you two to get a room."

"She doesn't want me in her life." The slice of her rejection still cut so much deeper than any other.

"Did she tell you that?"

"Very clearly," he said tightly, not enjoying in the least reliving the moment. "I think her words were along the lines of 'have a nice life.'"

"You've never been particularly self-aware."

He winced, closing down the computer file on his new maternity patient. "That's what she said."

"So are you going to continue to be a miserable ass or are you going to go out and meet Mari at the clinic gate?"

At the gate? He creaked upright in his chair, swinging his feet to the floor. "What the hell are you talking about? You're in Australia."

But he stormed over to look out his office window anyway.

"Sure, but you tasked me with her security and I figured some follow-up was in order. I've been keeping track of her with a combo of guards and a good old-fashioned GPS on her rental car. If my satellite connection is any good, she should be arriving right about... now."

Rowan spotted an SUV rounding the corner into sight, headlights sweeping the road as the vehicle drove toward the clinic. Could it really be Mari? Here? Suddenly, Elliot's call made perfect sense. He'd been stringing Rowan along on the line until just the right moment.

"And Rowan," Elliot continued, "be sure you're the one to say the whole 'love you' part first since she came to you. Merry Christmas, brother."

Love her?

Of course he loved her. Wanted her. Admired her. Desired her. Always had, and why he hadn't thought to tell her before now was incomprehensible to him. Thank God for his friends, who knew him well enough to boot him in the tail when he needed that nudge most.

Thank God for Mari, who hadn't given up on him. She challenged him. Disagreed with him. But yet here she was, for him.

The line disconnected as he was already out the door and sprinting down the hall, hand over his pager to keep it from dislodging from his scrubs in his haste. His gym shoes squeaked against the tiles as he turned the corner and burst out through the front door, into the starlit night. The brisk wind rippled his surgical scrubs.

The tan SUV parked beside the clinic's ambulance under a sprawling shea butter tree. The vehicle's dome light flicked on, and Merry Christmas to him, he saw Mari's beautiful face inside. She stepped out, one incredibly long leg at a time, wearing flowing silk pants and a tunic. The fabric glided along her skin the way his hands ached to do again.

Her appearance here gave him the first hope in nearly a week that he would get to do just that.

"You came," he said simply.

"Of course. It's Christmas." She walked toward him, the African night sky almost as magnificent as his princess. She wore the bracelets he'd given her, the bangles chiming against each other. Toe-to-toe, she stopped in front of him, the sweet scent and heat of her reaching out to him. "Where else would I be but with the man I l—"

He pressed a finger against her lips. "Wait, hold that thought. I have something I need to say first. I love you, Mariama Mandara. I've wanted you and yes, loved you, for longer than I can remember. And I will do whatever it takes to be worthy of your love in return."

"Ah, Rowan, don't you know? You're already exactly what I need and everything I want. God knows, if you get any more saintly you're likely to be raptured and I would miss you so very much. I love you, too."

Relief flooded him, his heart soaking up every word like the parched ground around him absorbing a rain shower. Unable to wait another second, he hauled her to his chest and kissed her, deeply, intensely, hoping she really understood just how much he meant those words. He loved her. The truth of that sang through him as tangibly as the carols carrying gently through an open window.

Ending the kiss with a nip to his bottom lip, Mari smiled up at him. "I had a far more eloquent speech planned. I even practiced saying it on the way over because I wanted the words to be as special as what we've shared together."

"I hope you trust I love you, too." He only wished he had a more romantic way of telling her.

"I do. You showed me." She tugged the ends of the stethoscope draped around his neck, her bracelets sliding along her arm. "I just needed to stop long enough to listen with my heart. And my heart says we're perfect for each other. That we're meant to be together."

"Then why did we give each other such a hard time all these years?"

"We are both smart, dedicated people with a lot to offer, but we should be challenged. It makes us better at what we do." She tugged his face closer, punctuating the words with a quick kiss. "And if I have my way, I'm going to challenge you every day for the rest of my life."

"You have mesmerized me since the moment I first saw you." Desire and love interlocked inside him, each spiking the other to a higher level.

"That's one of the things I love most about you." She toyed with his hair, which just brushed the collar of his scrubs.

"What would that be?" He looped his arms low around her waist.

"You think my baggy, wrinkled wardrobe is sexy."

"Actually, I think peeling the clothes off of you is life's most perfect pleasure." He brought them closer together, grateful to have her in his arms, determined never to let this woman slip away from him again.

"Well, then, Dr. Boothe, let's find somewhere private to go so you can unwrap your Christmas present."

* * * * *

*If you loved Rowan's story,
don't miss a single novel in*
THE ALPHA BROTHERHOOD *series from*
USA TODAY *bestselling author Catherine Mann:*

*AN INCONVENIENT AFFAIR
ALL OR NOTHING
PLAYING FOR KEEPS*

All available now from Harlequin Desire!

COMING NEXT MONTH FROM

HARLEQUIN®
Desire

Available November 5, 2013

#2263 THE SECRET HEIR OF SUNSET RANCH

The Slades of Sunset Ranch • by Charlene Sands

Rancher Justin Slade returns from war a hero...and finds out he's a father. But as things with his former fling heat back up, he must keep their child's paternity secret—someone's life depends on it.

#2264 TO TAME A COWBOY

Texas Cattleman's Club: The Missing Mogul
by Jules Bennett

When rodeo star Ryan Grant decides to hang up his spurs and settle down, he resolves to wrangle the heart of his childhood friend. But will she let herself be caught by this untamable cowboy?

#2265 CLAIMING HIS OWN

Billionaires and Babies • by Olivia Gates

Russian tycoon Maksim refuses to become like his abusive father, so he leaves the woman he loves and their son. But now he's returned a changed man...ready to stake his claim.

#2266 ONE TEXAS NIGHT...

Lone Star Legacy • by Sara Orwig

After a forbidden night of passion with his best friend's sister, Jared Weston gets a second chance. But can this risk taker convince the cautious Allison to risk it all on him?

#2267 EXPECTING A BOLTON BABY

The Bolton Brothers • by Sarah M. Anderson

One night with his investor's daughter shouldn't have led to more, but when she announces she's pregnant, real estate mogul Bobby Bolton must decide what's more important—family or money.

#2268 THE PREGNANCY PLOT

by Paula Roe

AJ wants a baby, and her ex is the perfect donor. But their simple baby plan turns complicated when Matt decides he wants a second chance with the one who got away!

———